MR. JANUARY

HEROES OF ROGUE VALLEY: CALENDAR GUYS
BOOK 1

ANN ROTH

OLIVER HEBER BOOKS

Copyright © 2015 Ann Roth

Published by Oliver-Heber Books

0 9 8 7 6 5 4 3 2 1

 Created with Vellum

INTRODUCTION

Welcome to Ann Roth's exciting new series, Heroes of Rogue Valley: Calendar Guys *series. Twelve months, 12 gorgeous firefighter heroes and the women who steal into their hearts and forever change their lives.*

Meet Mr. January:

Senior Firefighter Adam Healey is a man with a mission: get promoted to lieutenant at the Guff's Lake Fire Department. It's time, but more important, the promotion will finally earn him the respect of his dying father. Single mom Samantha Everett's deadbeat ex has left her to fend for herself, and she's working hard to support her young son with her baking business. Neither Adam nor Samantha is looking for a relationship. But love has a way of surprising people...

Mr. January–Adam Healey
    Age 30, 6' tall, 185 pounds
    Single
    Proud Senior Firefighter
    Time with Guff's Lake Fire Department: 9 years

1

A t the ungodly hour of five-forty-five a.m., Samantha Everett pulled into the delivery slot at Rosemary's Breakfast Nook. In the dark, the twin beams of the hatchback's headlights spotlighted the swirling snow. Well, it was early January in Rogue Valley.

"Please don't stick," she muttered under her breath, dreading the thought of putting on the tire chains.

Although so far, she hadn't needed them. When she'd moved to Guff's Lake six months earlier, locals had assured her that the usual winter temperatures tended to hover above freezing.

So different from the bone-chilling cold and frequent snowstorms in Enterprise.

"Look, Mom! Snow!" William chimed from the backseat.

At the age of five, he was delighted by almost everything—even at this hour. His joy was contagious, and Samantha's irritation dissipated like smoke. "I see it."

"Let me out." He unbuckled his car seat straps and bounced in anticipation for her to open the door.

Yawning—thanks to only five hours' sleep—Samantha exited the car. The building's perimeter lights cast long shadows across the nearly vacant concrete lot, a large area shared by several businesses. The few cars here now belonged to Rosemary, the cook, and wait staff. Rosemary's Breakfast Nook served the best breakfast in town, and snow or none, when the café opened at six, business would be brisk.

Despite the relative stillness, it was best to be safe. "Hold onto my coat," she directed.

Her itching-to-be-independent son grumbled but obeyed. Samantha opened the hatchback and jockeyed a dolly cart to the pavement. William helped her unfold it. Then she carefully loaded it with today's order—eight dozen still-warm cinnamon rolls, and six dozen each assorted muffins and scones. Her biggest order to date would net her more money than she'd ever earned as a baker in Enterprise.

Rosemary wouldn't pay her until a week from Friday, but Samantha had already divided and earmarked every penny. Groceries and other household expenses, bakery supplies, and the savings account for attorney fees.

To date, Jeff had ignored every one of the financial and custodial obligations spelled out in the divorce decree. Not one penny of child support or money for the debts he'd saddled her with, and not one request to see his son. Good riddance!

After all this time, Samantha doubted she'd ever hear from Jeff. She didn't need an attorney right now, but Betty Randall, her grandmotherly neighbor, believed that she did. Just in case. The woman had been so insistent Samantha had lost sleep over it. Mainly because Betty gave sound advice, unlike the unsolicited guidance from Samantha's parents.

William helped push the dolly toward the delivery entrance. As always, the door was unlocked for her, and easy to shoulder open and back through. Pausing inside the door, she brushed the snow off her son's parka and hat and then took care of her own coat.

The warmth, the fragrant aroma of freshly brewing coffee, and the haze from the sizzling vat of oil greeted her. A fragrant, smoky scent filled the air, and Samantha's mouth watered.

"Good morning," she greeted Rosemary and her longtime boyfriend and cook, José.

Round and perpetually cheerful, the forty-something restaurant owner greeted Samantha and William with her usual toothy smile. "Good morning." She winked at William. "How are you, sunshine?"

His small brow furrowed. "My name is William Tyler Everett Jones." Samantha had changed her last name back to Everett but had left her son's name intact.

From the time he'd first formed sentences, he'd insisted that everyone use his given name.

"I know that, darlin', but seeing you always makes me smile, and a true smile is as warm as the sunshine," Rosemary said. "Do you two have time for breakfast this morning?"

"Say yes, Mom." William gave Samantha the round-eyed, pleading look she'd never been able to resist.

Guff's Lake Bed & Breakfast, her only other paying client so far, didn't expect her until seven, and William's half-day kindergarten wouldn't start for several hours yet. She ought to use the time on housework—keeping the kitchen spotless was a constant chore.

But she really could use another cup of coffee and

something to eat besides the bowl of cold cereal waiting for her at home.

"We'd love to have breakfast here," she said. "Can I put in an order for José's hash browns?"

José chuckled. "You bet. Bacon and eggs, too?"

"Yes, please."

"And cocoa?" William asked, going all round-eyed again.

Rosemary nodded. "I'll bring it with your breakfast."

As she filled a coffee mug for Samantha, Jana, one of the waitresses and Samantha's best friend, entered the kitchen through the restaurant's swinging doors.

"I thought I heard you in here. Can you believe it's snowing? I'll bet you love that, William. Let's get the case loaded."

Samantha wheeled the dolly to the counter out front, where bright walls and colorful posters added a homey, cheerful feel to the restaurant. She and William kept Jana company while she arranged Samantha's baked goods in the case and placed the printed "Treats by Samantha" sign in plain view. What didn't fit stayed in the delivery boxes for restocking the case until the restaurant closed at one.

Rosemary inspected the finished display with a satisfied nod. "You and William go on and make yourselves at home," she told Samantha. "I'll bring your food out shortly."

Samantha let her son choose where to sit. He led her to his favorite spot, a booth in front of the big picture window that faced the door. With the restaurant minutes from opening, Jana and the three other servers bustled around, seeing to last-minute details. Then one of the waitresses unlocked the door and welcomed in the morning's first customers.

Moments later, Rosemary delivered breakfast to Samantha and William. While Samantha enjoyed her food and coffee, her son chattered nonstop. During recess at Guff's Lake Elementary, the school he proudly called his own, he would have a snowball fight and build a snowman with Douglas and Harper, his two best friends.

Customers steadily streamed in to eat at the restaurant or collect their breakfast and morning coffee to go, some alone, others in groups. The almost twenty thousand Guff's Lake residents tended to be a friendly bunch, and even the people Samantha didn't recognize greeted her with nods and smiles.

Sipping a second cup of coffee and staring out the window with relief as the snow let up, she watched an orange 4Runner pull into the lot. A solid-looking male slid out of the driver's seat. Dressed in a leather bomber jacket, jeans, and a baseball cap, he wore a cast on one foot and a sling on his arm. A backpack swung from the other shoulder. Even with his arm injury and hobbling gait, he managed to move with a purposeful stride that for some reason reminded her of a big, sleek jungle cat. A tiger or a puma came to mind.

The sky had lightened a fraction, and between the approaching dawn and the perimeter lights, she easily made out his face.

And oh, what a face! The broad forehead, strong chin, and straight nose only added to his overall attractiveness. With a jolt of awareness, she recognized him. Adam Healey, aka Mr. January in the Guff's Lake Fire Department calendar that had come out last month, just in time for Christmas, as part of an ongoing fund-raising drive for the fire department's benefit fund.

The calendar featured twelve of the most gorgeous men Samantha had ever laid eyes on, and listed fascinating information, including height, weight, and marital status. She recalled that Adam was single.

Every female in town, along with a host of men and all the local businesses, had purchased calendars. At Rosemary's Breakfast Nook, the calendar hung prominently in the display case, with Adam in his firefighter hat, grinning and shirtless under a deep blue sky. In the background, the snowy Siskiyou Mountains. Samantha glanced at it and blew out an admiring sigh.

Everyone knew that the guys from the Guff's Lake Fire Department hung out here, since the station a was mere two blocks away. Ordinarily Samantha came and went before any of them wandered in for coffee and breakfast. But today...

Adam must have sensed her staring at him, for his gaze met hers through the window. Embarrassed, she turned her attention to William.

"—read more *Charlotte's Web* to us today," he said, still chattering about his kindergarten class.

"That's such a great book," she replied.

The door opened, and a gust of cold air rushed in. But the man who shut it behind him sucked the chill right out of the room.

Adam's eyes were still riveted on her. She couldn't seem to tear her glance away, either. Up this close, his pale-blue eyes were even more striking than they were in the calendar photo. The color of the sky just before the sun rose.

It had been a while since a man turned her head, and she wasn't sure she liked that fluttery feeling of attraction. She'd moved here to escape Enterprise and the past and start fresh, and for the first time in more than three years, she was happy. Between taking care of William and supporting the two of them with her baked-goods business, socializing with friends and a weekly knitting class, she had filled her life to the brim. She didn't have time to look at a man, let alone date.

Or so she assured herself.

Ready to leave, she pushed to her feet and stacked her breakfast dishes to make cleanup easier for Jana. Her friend sashayed toward Adam with her hips swaying and a longing look on her face.

Jana was dating someone, but she wasn't blind. By the similar expressions the other waitresses wore, they were just as smitten. So were the other women in the café, who checked Adam out with approval.

"Hey there, Adam," Jana said with a flirty smile. "I didn't expect to see you this early in the morning. How are that wrist and ankle?"

"Getting better every day."

"Adam!" Rosemary bustled over with a grin on her face. "You're just in time to meet Samantha Everett, the bakery goddess behind Samantha's Treats, the goodies that bring you back every morning. Adam's a huge fan," she told Samantha.

"That's right. Hey." He touched the bill of his hat.

He was a big man, a good six inches taller than Samantha and powerfully built. Even wearing ankle boots that added two inches to her five-feet-six-inch height, she felt small.

"Hi," she answered, cupping her empty mug to her chest. As if it could deflect the mesmerizing warmth in his eyes.

"William, this is Adam Healey," Rosemary continued. "He's a firefighter."

"For real?" Her son looked starstruck.

"How you doing, sport?" Adam asked.

"My name is William Tyler Everett Jones."

"That's quite a mouthful. Mind if I call you sport?"

"Okay."

This was a first, and surprised Samantha.

Adam sniffed. "I smell smoke."

Right then, a waitress hurried out of the kitchen balancing several plates. Wisps of smoke followed her. The smoke alarm screeched, and people stopped eating.

"Everyone, clear out," Adam ordered in a booming voice. "Keep an eye on this." He handed his backpack to Samantha. On his way to the kitchen he pulled his arm from the sling, whipped out his phone and made a call.

"What's that noise? Where is he going, Mom?" William asked as he and Samantha donned their coats and headed toward the door.

"To see what set off the smoke detector."

"Why can't we go with him?"

"We don't want to get in the way. Besides, we need to get going." But she had Adam's backpack and she'd left her dolly behind the display case.

She would have handed the backpack to someone and come back later for the dolly, but her son dug in his heels. "I want to wait and see what happens," he said, his breath clouding in the cold.

The stubborn set of his jaw reminded her of Jeff when they were still married. Before he'd walked away from her and William, just days before her twenty-seventh birthday. The last time William had seen his father, he'd been all of twenty-six months old. Yet somehow, he'd picked up that stubborn look.

Getting him into the car without a battle wouldn't be easy, and Samantha didn't have the energy for an argument. With a sigh, she nodded and waited out front with the other restaurant patrons.

∼

A BURNER HAD CAUGHT FIRE, and thick smoke rapidly filled the kitchen. Adam grabbed the fire extinguisher and went to work. In seconds, he had the flames out.

"Open the back door and get some fresh air in here," he directed.

Rosemary complied, and José swiped his brow. "That was close. I shouldn't have set that towel so close to the flames. It won't happen again."

Adam nodded. "Hang on while I call the station." He made the call then disconnected. "They're coming anyway. It's what we do."

His sprained wrist hurt like hell. Should've been more careful when he'd hefted the extinguisher. But his focus had been on putting out the fire before something really bad happened, and he'd forgotten to think about himself.

He started to massage it, winced, and slipped it back into the sling. With any luck, it would continue to mend, and he could start light duty next week. Eight hours a day, five days a week, doing filing and other administrative work. Not his job of choice. He preferred working a pair of back-to-back, twenty-four-hour shifts, fighting fires, or serving as a paramedic. Still, light duty beat sitting at home, twiddling his thumbs, and trying to study. The two weeks he'd just suffered through was more than enough time off.

"When did you last have a fire and life safety training refresher?" he asked Rosemary.

"I'm not sure. Maybe a year? Do you remember, José?"

"I'd say more like two."

This year, Nate was in charge of safety training, and Adam made a mental note to let him know to schedule something here. For all he knew, Nate might be on the engine today. Since Adam had been forced to take disability leave, he'd lost track of who did what this month.

"Let's clean up this mess and get back to work," Rosemary said.

José nodded. "I'll toss everything I was cooking, and start over."

"I'll let our customers know," Rosemary said. "Adam, how about coffee and a treat on the house?"

He couldn't argue with that. "A scone and an espresso sound good. Make it a double. I need the extra caffeine. This studying is a real bear."

Rosemary frowned. "What are you studying for?"

"The exam I need to pass so I can get promoted to lieutenant." That was the next rung up from senior firefighter and one rank below captain. Adam already knew a lot of what he needed for the job, but the class he'd enrolled in focused on management skills, which he didn't have. He'd made it more than halfway through the sixteen-week course, but there was still a lot to learn before the written test in late February. The class and the studying were rougher than he'd expected.

He returned to the restaurant and watched the diners file inside again.

In the midst of that, Rafe, Daniel, Hank, and Max strode in, just as Adam had known they would. Big men, decked out in fire gear.

"Like I told you, it's been handled," Adam greeted them.

"You know the drill," Adam's best bud, Rafe, replied.

Adam's crewmates tromped into the kitchen to make sure the fire was out and check for fire within the walls.

Samantha and her kid returned to their booth. She handed him his backpack.

"Mind if join you?" Adam asked.

When the little guy grinned, she shrugged. "Okay.

Adam slid in beside him, putting him across from Samantha. He'd heard about her—divorced, moved to Guff's Lake six months ago, house-sitting Lucy Marks's place while the older woman wintered in Palm Desert.

She was a looker—short black hair, long, wispy bangs, big eyes, and a sexy mouth that made him think of pleasure. But he didn't get involved with single mothers. He never had, mainly because most of them were looking for husbands. And judging by the relationships Adam had screwed up, he figured he'd make a lousy husband and father.

"Was it a big fire?" the boy asked. He had his mother's eyes.

"It could have been," Adam said. "But it's all good now."

William nodded somberly. "What happened to your arm and leg?"

Adam shrugged. "I hurt them fighting a fire." With his wrist still screaming, he figured he'd set himself back. That really teed him off, and not only because he wanted back on regular duty. Until he healed, he couldn't take the physical exam he needed to qualify for lieutenant.

Between the management class, the written and physical exams, and the interview, the whole process would take roughly four months. Time he couldn't afford to make up later, not if he wanted his father to see him promoted.

To finally make him proud. Adam wanted that just about more than he'd ever wanted anything.

His buds returned to the restaurant, stopping at the booth where Adam sat.

Every one of them looked Samantha over.

"Hello. I'm Rafe Donato." Flashing the twin dimples that had women falling all over him, Rafe shook her hand.

"This is Samantha and her son, William," Adam said by way of introduction. "I just met them myself. Samantha makes all that stuff in the front case."

"So you're the talent behind those scones. I'm Max Meier."

Max also shook her hand. Women said his brown eyes were soulful, and Samantha looked as if she bought that hook, line, and sinker.

Adam didn't like it, but what did he care? "These two other guys are Daniel and Hank."

Lanky Daniel grinned, and Hank, the station's newest and most solemn firefighter, nodded.

Each of them shook hands with her kid, who was all eyes.

Other diners came over to say hello. Adam didn't miss the looks women gave him and his buds. They were used to that.

A moment later, Rafe checked his watch. "We're a little over an hour until the end of our second shift. We should go."

The crew's back-to-back shifts started at eight a.m. on Mondays and ended at eight a.m. on Wednesdays, when another crew took over.

"Good to meet you, William. Samantha." Rafe

nodded to Rosemary and the waitresses. "I'll see you ladies for breakfast shortly."

As they filed out, Adam swore he heard collective female sighs.

Although Samantha seemed immune to his crewmates' charms. Adam wasn't about to examine why he felt relieved.

"We should leave now, too," Samantha said. "We still have another delivery to make, and then William needs to get ready for school."

Already standing, the boy cupped his groin and danced from foot to foot. "Mom, I gotta pee."

Samantha gave Adam a Kids, what can you do? look and then slid quickly from the booth. "Hurry, before you have an accident."

"I don't wanna use the girls' bathroom."

"Well, I can't go into the men's."

"I'll take him," Adam offered.

Unsure whether she should trust this man she'd just met with her son, Samantha hesitated. "That isn't necessary."

"I gotta go right now," William insisted.

"He's a good guy," Janna added from a nearby table, where she was pouring coffee.

Samantha relaxed. Anyway, there was no time to argue. Adam ferried her son toward the men's room. "Sit tight, Sam," he said over his shoulder. "We'll be right back."

SAM. Adam had called her Sam. Samantha sat back in the booth and sighed. She didn't go by the shortened version of her name anymore, hadn't since high school. Even her parents called her Samantha.

She kind of liked hearing it again on Adam's lips. Not that she was interested in him. She wasn't, she assured herself.

By the time he brought her son back, she was up and waiting with her coat on and holding out William's.

"Thanks, Adam." She helped her son into his parka.

"No prob. Be good, sport."

"I will."

"Hey, I'll be back at work next week. If you ever want to visit the fire station, give me a call and I'll show you two around." Adam wrote his cell number on the back of his card.

"Really?" William looked as if it was Christmas morning.

Samantha preferred to steer clear of the firefighter she was attracted to, but she couldn't bear to disappoint her son. "We just might take you up on that."

A tour to please William, and that would be that. As they headed toward the car, she pushed the firefighter from her thoughts.

2

W

ednesday morning, Adam crossed the
walkway of the bungalow where his father lived, just as he did each morning on
his days off. Nella, the home health nurse, had already
come and gone. As usual, she'd tacked a note for
Adam on the front door. His father was stable, had
taken his meds and been shaved, washed, and fed.

Adam knocked once. Without waiting for a reply,
he wiped his feet on the mat and walked into the
living room.

The same faded drapes that had hung on the
window since the old man had moved in after the divorce some fifteen years ago were drawn against the
weak sun. Adam figured Nella had attempted to pull
them open and the old man had ordered them left
closed, preferring darkness and gloom.

Sprawled in his La-Z-Boy in front of the tube, he
was watching the Today show. The TV tray with its
pitcher of fresh water, a glass and straw were within
easy reach. Nasal cannula, the tubes that fed his body
the air his lungs could provide only on a limited basis,
rhythmically sucked precious oxygen from a nearby
cylinder.

"Hey, Pop." Favoring his uninjured arm and foot, Adam sat down carefully on the saggy couch against the wall. "How you doing this morning?"

Frowning, his father muted the TV. "As shitty as ever."

Emphysema caused by his pack-a-day habit and smoke inhalation from fires he'd battled before the SCBA—self-contained breathing apparatus—had become mandatory, had stolen his ability to speak as much as he once had. But the bitterness had been with him for sixteen years now, since the day life had thrown a curve ball that had destroyed the family forever.

Now he was dying. He hadn't touched alcohol in five years. Shortly after his diagnosis three years ago, he'd also quit cigarettes. By then, it'd been too late. The doctor had given him eight months, max.

The old man still had an appetite, though. Eyeing the red, black, and gold Rosemary's Breakfast Nook logo on the bag Adam had brought from the café when he'd stopped for breakfast earlier, he licked his lips. "You going to give me that, or what?"

Adam pushed to his feet, stifling a pained grimace as his wrist and ankle hollered at him to tread lightly. He dropped the bag on the TV table.

Without ceremony or thanks, the old man opened it and pulled out the blueberry muffin tucked inside. His favorite. The oxygen cylinder tick-tick-ticked as he ate the entire thing. When he finished, he sat back, wiped his mouth, and briefly closed his eyes.

"Yesterday, I met the woman who makes those things. Samantha Everett," Adam said.

"Is that so?" For the first time this morning, interest gleamed in his father's eyes. "What's she like?"

"She's about my age, with a five-year-old son."

"Married, then."

Adam shook his head. "Divorced."

"Like you and me."

Adam's divorce had been nothing like his father's. Grief, bitterness, and booze had destroyed his parents' marriage. Adam's had failed because he'd been too young and had done stupid things.

"Is she built?" With his hands, his father air-sketched a curvy body.

"Pop." Adam rolled his eyes.

"Well?"

"She's not bad."

Understatement of the year. Adam remembered the way Sam's jeans had hugged her slender legs, and the red pullover sweater that had clung to her ample breasts. He swallowed.

Over the past twenty-four hours, he'd thought about her way too much. It was a relief that by the time he'd ventured into Rosemary's this morning, she'd already left.

His father gave him a shrewd look. "That good, huh?" He shook his head and chuckled. "I'll bet she didn't look twice at the likes of you."

Usual Richard Healey fare, and Adam barely cringed. "You didn't ask, but the management class and studying are going okay."

"I didn't ask because I don't understand why you're wasting your time and money."

He still didn't believe Adam had the smarts to get promoted. Determined to prove him wrong, Adam straightened up tall. "You'll see, Pop. Someday, I'll make captain, just like you did."

Wearing the wistful look that signaled he was back in the past, Richard didn't appear to have heard. No doubt, he was thinking about the good old days. Before he'd lost himself in a bottle.

Before Marcus.

"Your brother would have made a fine lieutenant...."

Did he have to bring up Marcus every freaking day? The question crowded Adam's throat, but he bit the words back. Although his brother had been gone sixteen years, since Adam was fourteen and Marcus was seventeen, his father was still in mourning.

For years, Adam had been, too. He'd worshipped his big brother and missed him to this day. He always would. In a strange way, he blamed himself for Marcus's untimely death. But life went on, and over time, Adam had realized that no one was to blame.

He'd moved past the tragedy. Except when he visited his father. Then the guilt set in and the regret for his own mistakes. For having been a handful of a kid and causing all kinds of trouble—in contrast to Marcus, the golden boy and the apple of their daddy's eye.

If Adam had been a better son, toeing the line and making decent grades instead of barely skating by, maybe his father would have stayed sober after Marcus's death instead of drinking himself into a stupor every night. He wouldn't have taken early retirement from his job as captain of the Guff's Lake Fire Department. He might even still be married to Adam's mom.

Not that Adam begrudged his mother for remarrying. She and Jack had been happily married for ten years now and had relocated to Carmel, California.

The old man had never remarried. Once he'd retired, he'd stayed drunk most of the time. It was a wonder he'd made it this long.

His father returned to his show and upped the volume to extra-loud.

In other words, dismissed, over and out.

What else was new? He'd never especially liked Adam and certainly had never respected him.

But if Adam made lieutenant.... He wanted to make his father proud. Just once before he died. So he could fix this one, pivotal relationship he'd ruined.

He had to get that promotion.

"I'll see you tomorrow," he said over the TV.

His father's attention never strayed from the screen. He made a dismissive gesture. "Suit yourself. Be sure to bring me a muffin."

"ARE you sure you have time for this?" Jana asked as Samantha slowed to avoid a pothole on Kirkdale Road, one of the few roads that ran from one end of town to the other.

Despite the gray day, the rolling, winter-brown fields, scattered homes, and distant Siskiyou Mountains made for a pretty drive.

Since it was Thursday, Jana's day off, they were headed to Deb's Knitting Store on the south side of town for their weekly knitting lesson.

"Probably not, but if I don't do something besides bake and take care of William, I swear, I'll wither up and die," Samantha admitted. "Besides, the sweater I started last week needs serious help. I've ripped out the stitches twice so far, and I probably need to rip them out again. At this rate, I won't finish until summer." She gestured at the knitting bag in the backseat. "See for yourself."

Jana pivoted, grabbed the bag, and put it on her lap. She pulled out the lopsided mess. "Love the soft yellow, but you weren't kidding. This is pretty bad."

What could Samantha do but laugh? "Eventually, I'll get it right."

"That's what I admire about you. Once you make up your mind to do something, you stick with it. I wish I could be more like that."

They were approaching Guff's Lake now, the city's namesake. Nestled in the foothills of the Siskiyou Mountains, the spectacular natural lake and the trails, woods, and resort around it, drew tourists and locals alike for hiking and fishing.

"You definitely don't want to be like me," Samantha replied. "You get a regular paycheck and all those tips. Plus you're dating a guy you really like."

Uncharacteristically silent, Jana studied the ends of her shoulder-length, blonde hair—a sure sign something bothered her.

Uh-oh. As Samantha braked for a red light, a light drizzle began to fall. "Don't tell me. You and Jon broke up."

"Not yet. He even brought me out here to the lake the other night."

"In the winter? Wow. I'm impressed. Are you saying he kissed you under the ash tree?"

Local folklore claimed that if a couple kissed under the lofty, centuries-old ash tree growing half a dozen yards from the lake, they would find true and lasting love.

"That could've been his plan, but we never even made it out of the car before things got hot and heavy. We ended up rushing back to my house. He stayed over." Jana bit her lip. "You know that means it's only a matter of time before we break up."

The light turned green, and Samantha drove on. "I thought this time you were going to wait awhile."

"Yeah, but I couldn't help myself." Jana gave a

what-can-you-do shrug. "That's another thing I admire about you. You have a lot more self-control around men."

"It has nothing to do with self-control. If you'd suffered through what I did, you wouldn't want anything to do with dating or relationships, either." Although after meeting Adam Healey the other day, Samantha had begun to rethink that.

No. She wasn't. She had a son to raise and a business to grow. Not to mention an ex out there, who could show up at any time to claim his parental rights. After nearly three years without any contact from Jeff, however, that seemed unlikely. All the same, Samantha's stomach tightened into a worried knot.

"Have you talked to an attorney yet?" Jana asked, as if she'd read Samantha's mind. "You should. The sooner, the better."

"You sound like Betty Randall. I agree, and I will hire someone, but I doubt waiting a few more months will make much difference. Except to me. I want to have enough saved to pay the attorney fee up front."

"Do me a favor and find someone anyway. They might let you make monthly payments. Getting the ball rolling will cut out some of the stress in your life."

After struggling for three years to pay the bills she and Jeff had piled up during their three-year marriage —and was still paying on several—Samantha had sworn off debt of any kind. "I admit I sometimes worry about Jeff showing up someday. But he's been out of the picture for nearly as long as our marriage lasted. I doubt he'll show up anytime soon, or even at all."

And yet, some sixth sense warned her not to get caught off-guard.

They were almost at the knitting shop before Jana spoke again. "You may have sworn off men, but after

what happened at breakfast the other morning...."
She fanned herself.

Samantha frowned. "What are you talking about?"

"You and Adam Healey. You just about swooned, and he seemed pretty darn interested, too."

"No, I didn't," Samantha protested. "As for Adam, I watched his stuff while he dealt with the fire. Then Rosemary offered him a free coffee and snack, and he happened to sit down with us. End of story."

"Well, he sure didn't check me out, or anyone else except you. What's the harm, Samantha? Adam's gorgeous, and he's a decent guy. Besides, you're single, he's single...."

"As it is, I barely have time for sleep. Our knitting lessons are my one indulgence. And don't forget about William."

"I know, I know. You're focused on him and your business. At least take Adam up on his offer to show you and William around the fire station."

"I plan to, sometime next week." Relieved to see the sign for Deb's Knitting Store just ahead, Samantha signaled and slowed down. "Here we are."

She pulled into the small parking lot in front of the building and maneuvered into a space.

Determined to forget all about Adam Healey, she grabbed her knitting and headed inside for an hour of fun and relaxation.

3

When it came to boring, data entry ranked down there with scrubbing toilets. Seated at the station's computer desk in the main floor business office, Adam rolled his shoulders. After hours at the hunt-and-peck chore, his wrist throbbed and his eyes were starting to cross.

Not that he was complaining. Being at the station again, hanging with the captain and the eleven other crewmates he loved and trusted like brothers, felt good. Living together forty-eight hours a week and watching each other's backs during fires and medical calls had bonded them tighter than most people ever got.

Bonus: the rest of the week was theirs to fill any way they chose.

Thanks to his injuries, Adam's schedule this week was Monday, Wednesday, Friday from ten to six. After this week and until the doctor cleared him for regular duty, he'd work a straight Monday through Friday, forty-hour week. Adam wasn't thrilled with the temporary schedule, but hell, he was lucky to be here at all. Only because he'd assured Kent Comings, his shift's captain, that his wrist had all but healed.

For that reason, he'd ditched the sling and the Ace bandage and used both hands on the keyboard. Now he was paying for fudging the truth. The swelling in his wrist looked the way it had before he'd arrived at the station, which counted for something. Aspirin should take care of the pain. Adam popped two tabs, dry.

At the moment, the building was quiet. Only he, Patty, the station's the fire marshal, and the admin staff were around. Everyone else had gone out—three on a medical call and seven plus the captain on a fire call. The other two were at one of the local retirement homes, conducting the fire and safety classes the crew took turns teaching.

Missing the action and tired of sitting around, he stood, stretched and sauntered to the front desk, where the secretary, Miranda, kept an eye on people who wandered in. "I'm taking a break," he told her.

Hands flying over the keyboard, she smiled and nodded. "Enjoy."

Not likely. His injuries prevented him from the weekly physical training sessions, the daily workouts in the gym upstairs, or participating in the mandatory inventory and equipment checks the rest of the crew performed each morning. As sidelined as a firefighter could be.

Adam thought about hitting the books for fifteen minutes, but studying was almost as bad as data entry. Lieutenants had a lot more paperwork than the fire-fighters they managed.

Did he really want this promotion?

Hell, yeah, both to make his pop proud and be-cause he was ready to move into management.

Maybe he'd limp over to Rosemary's and grab a

coffee. As he headed to his locker to grab his jacket, his cell phone buzzed.

He slid it from his pocket and checked the screen. Samantha Everett. Huh. It'd been over a week since that morning at Rosemary's, but he still thought about her.

"Adam Healey," he said, not wanting her to know he'd input her name and number the day they'd met.

"It's Samantha Everett. The one who makes the baked goods?" She sounded stiff and nervous.

"Hey."

"Hi. Um, William has been at me day and night to visit the fire station. Is it okay to bring him over after his nap this afternoon? If you're not too busy on your first day back."

Adam liked that she remembered that, liked the idea of showing her and William around. Way too much. Because he wanted to give the kid the thrill of seeing the trucks and rescue vehicles up close, he told himself. "I have time. How about fifteen hundred hours? That's military time for three o'clock."

"Perfect."

Two hours later, the whole crew had returned to the station and gathered in the apparatus bay, aka the garage, readying the vehicles and their personal stuff for the next call. Liam, Owen, Tony, Rob, and Ethan checked the equipment on the fire truck. Daniel, Gus, and Hank gathered in the small biohazard room to clean the medical equipment used on the most recent paramedic call, while Nate, Rafe, and Max put the ambulance to rights. Captain Comings logged data into the computer call log. Needing another break from the computer, Adam joined them.

Suddenly, the in-house intercom squawked to life, signaling an announcement rather than a call from the 911 dispatch serving both the fire and police departments. "Adam, you have visitors," Miranda said.

His buds eyed him curiously.

"It's for a tour around the station," he explained, his eagerness to see Sam making his voice gruff.

Ignoring his sore ankle, he strode toward the entry area with barely a limp. He found Sam and William checking out the station's first fire truck, circa 1913, displayed in the center of the visitor area.

In the seconds before they noticed him, Adam studied Sam. Short, shiny black hair framing her face, with long, wispy bangs. Big, pretty eyes, lit with the obvious joy she took in her son's excitement. Her heavy, knee-length coat hung open, revealing a bright blue turtleneck sweater over jeans, and ankle boots.

She looked good, real good.

As soon as he formed the thought, she glanced up and caught him checking her out. Her cheeks flushed prettily, and, for a moment, he couldn't look away.

Then William spotted him. "Adam!"

Sam laughed. "He's pretty excited."

"So I see. Hey, sport." Adam ruffled the boy's hair, which was as black as his mother's, but not as shiny. He gestured to the coat tree in the corner. "Why don't you hang up your jackets?"

They did.

He didn't have much experience with five-year-olds, but they all liked visiting the apparatus bay. "Ready to look around the station?"

The boy beamed and nodded.

Adam nodded at the tote on the floor beside Sam. "We can store that for you while you take the tour."

"Actually, these are for you and whoever else is here."

She handed the bag to Adam. Right away, he

smelled something good. "Scones," he said, licking his lips.

"And muffins. My way of thanking you for taking the time to show us around."

He couldn't believe she'd brought treats for him and everyone. No woman had ever done that, not even his ex when they'd been dating.

Miranda opened the window of the glass barrier where she sat and stuck her head out. "What you got there, Adam?"

"Scones and muffins," Sam said, smiling at her. "There's one in here for you, too. I'm Samantha Everett."

"Miranda Zindell. You're the one who makes those yummy goodies they sell at Rosemary's. Thanks to you, my diet is forever ruined, but what a way to go," she said good naturedly. Moments later, she joined Adam in the entry area and helped herself.

Captain Comings and Fire Marshal Johnson headed toward Sam. "Did someone say muffins and scones?" Captain Comings said.

Adam made the introductions, and the two high-ups helped themselves.

"We'll pass out the rest of these as we go," Adam said.

News traveled fast, and by then, Erin, the station's HR specialist, and everyone else knew about Sam's gift. As they flocked around her and murmured appreciatively, Adam introduced her and William to the guys she hadn't met yet. Grins bloomed on every face, even Hank's solemn mug.

She'd made a big hit, and not just for the treats. Her sparkling eyes and big smile lit up the station.

A couple of the guys really checked her out. Adam didn't like that. She'd brought William here for a tour, not a flirt session. At his warning frown, his crewmates quickly returned to their tasks.

Adam disposed of the empty bag then turned to William, who had noted everything with interest. "Let's head for the apparatus bay. That's a fancy way of saying 'garage', where we keep all our vehicles." Once there, he posed a question sure to delight the boy. "Whenever we get a call, we have to move fast. Do you want to see how we quickly get from the second floor, where we eat and sleep, all the way down here?"

"Yeah," William said.

Adam showed him the brass pole housed in a small room off the apparatus bay. "We slide down this."

The little boy's eyes almost popped out of his head. "Can I try?"

Sam looked as if she wanted to try, too. Adam gave his head a slight shake.

"I wish you both could, but it's against regulations."

"How come?"

"It's not safe for kids. Years ago, a boy about your age tried to shinny up. Unfortunately, he couldn't hold on. He fell and broke his leg."

William's eyes widened further. "Wow."

"Let's look at the vehicles in here." Adam pointed out the different fire trucks, the rescue cars, and the ambulance. "Ever been on a fire truck?" As he'd expected, William shook his head. "How would you like to sit in the right front seat?"

His seat if he got promoted to lieutenant. *When,* not *if,* he silently amended.

The boy's jaw dropped. "Can I?"

"If your mom okays it."

"Of course." Sam's eyes telegraphed she was pleased.

They sure were pretty. Green, with flecks of gold in them, the kind a man could lose himself in. But with his nosey buds just waiting for a chance to razz him about Sam....

Adam turned to her son. "Up you go, sport." He made a step out of his hands and boosted the little guy up.

Then William sat up in the seat, straining to see out a window that was too high for him. The kid looked cute up there.

Adam explained about the computer screen between the two front seats, and how it provided information, including maps and driving routes. Not that he or the other guys ever relied on the computer for the best route anywhere. The engineer and the man in the right seat kept the information stored in their heads.

Liam ambled over. He was a stand-up guy, but his shaved head, huge frame, and fierce expression tended to intimidate those who didn't know him. William chewed his lip.

Adam elbowed his bud. "Smile, will ya? You're scaring the kid."

Immediately, Liam's scowl lifted into a grin, transforming his face. "Hey, William. Thanks again for the muffin. In case you forgot, I'm Liam. I'm an engineer— the guy who drives this rig."

"Oh." His fears forgotten, the kid looked thoughtful. "How come you don't drive, Adam?"

Liam chuckled. "It's not as easy at it looks. I spent quite awhile, getting qualified to do it."

"That's right," Adam added. "On our shift, there

are two engineers. Liam is one of them, and the other is Max. Remember him?"

William nodded. "He came to the restaurant after you put out the fire. And he ate his scone today really fast."

"Cute kid," Liam told Sam.

"He is, isn't he?" She smiled fondly at her son.

Her open show of love for the boy touched Adam. William was a lucky kid, luckier than Adam had been at that age. At any age. Most of his parents' love and affection had gone to Marcus, with Adam coming in a distant second. Even after Marcus had passed on.

Suddenly, the distinct voice of Sarah McCone, one of the dispatchers, filled the air, announcing a call.

"Gotta go," Liam said. "Next time."

Adam doubted there would be a next time. He didn't plan on seeing Sam or William again.

Adrenaline pumping as it did whenever a call came through dispatch, he steered his visitors into the hall, out of the way of the crew, where guys were suiting up with the clothing they'd laid out on the floor near the aid cars and fire truck. "You can watch from here."

"Why is Liam putting on those clothes?" William asked as Liam quickly pulled on his shirt, pants and suspenders, then bent to lace up his steel-toe boots.

"It's called turnout gear, and it will help protect him from the fire."

As Liam and the three men riding with him jumped into their seats, the big garage doors rolled open. The truck headed out, its siren shrilling before it even reached the street. An aid car followed.

"That was exciting," Samantha said as the sound of the siren faded away.

Adam agreed. He hated being sidelined, but he

couldn't do anything about that. And Sam and William were waiting.

"Ready to see the rest of the station?" he asked.

"THANKS, ADAM," Samantha said some thirty minutes after the fire truck and aid car had whisked the firefighters away. William had insisted on using the bathroom by himself, and she and Adam were waiting for him outside the men's room of the station. "This tour meant a lot to my son." She'd had a great time meeting everyone and spending time with Adam. He was good with William, treating him like a person instead of a little boy to be ignored. "I enjoyed it, too," she added.

"So did I." He almost sounded surprised.

His pale-blue eyes warmed and settled on her mouth. As if he wanted to kiss her. That would be a very bad idea, Samantha told herself, but her body wouldn't listen. Her nerves hummed, and she had to fight the urge to lean in and let him. Hoping William would hurry out of the bathroom, she pulled his parka from the coat tree.

To her relief, Adam's cell phone rang, and his focus changed. He checked the screen, and with a look she couldn't read, answered. "Hey, Nella."

Signaling that he'd be right back, he stepped away, out of earshot.

He was involved with someone named Nella.

Well, shoot. Samantha was disappointed but not surprised. A smart, handsome, sexy guy like Adam was bound to have a girlfriend. Anyway, she didn't want or have time for a man in her life.

Yet the way he'd looked at her....

By the time Adam returned, she'd pulled herself together.

"That was my father's day nurse," he said.

"Oh?" Samantha frowned. "Is he sick?"

"He has emphysema, and he's having a bad day," he said. "Nella's going to take him to see his doctor."

"Will he be okay?"

"Temporarily." Adam scrubbed his hand over his very short hair.

Samantha felt for him. Even though her parents had urged her to forgive Jeff for cheating on her and advised her to "win" him back, which made her furious every time she thought about it, she still loved them. She felt lucky they were both strong and healthy. "I'm sorry."

"It is what it is." Adam checked his watch, then glanced at the men's room door. "William's been in there awhile. Maybe I should check on him."

Her son chose that moment to exit the bathroom.

"Are you okay?" Samantha asked.

He nodded. "I washed my hands and everything!"

Adam's grim expression lightened. He chuckled, the sound rusty, as if he hadn't made it in a good long time. "Good job, sport."

"I'm hungry, Mom," William said.

"Which is why we're leaving right now. It's time to start dinner. Do you have anything to say to Adam, William?"

"Thank you."

Adam nodded. "My pleasure."

Samantha helped her son into his coat and then shrugged into her own. As she exited the building, she felt Adam's eyes on her.

———

4

Without knowing quite how it happened, Adam found himself ducking against the icy sleet that pummeled his head and shoulders and quickly climbing the steps to the covered porch of Sam's place. He'd last seen her on Monday, three days ago. On this, his final Thursday off until he started his five-days-a-week light duty, he'd met a couple of the guys at Rosemary's for breakfast. Then he'd stopped at the old man's to deliver a muffin and try to make nice. That hadn't gone well, but it never did.

Now here he was, knocking on the door of the house that had been built a century ago by the wealthy orchard owner Byron Marks, and had passed through the family to his great-granddaughter, Lucy. Adam had never been inside, but everyone in town knew that Lucy had spent a good deal of her considerable fortune to keep the place in tip-top shape.

As he blew on his cold hands to warm them, an older woman clutching an umbrella strolled by and blatantly checked him out.

"Morning," he called out.

"Good morning." She smiled and continued on, disappearing around the corner.

Sam opened the door, wearing a distracted look. She'd pinned her bangs back with a silver clip, for all the good it did. Most of the strands had escaped. Water darkened the cuff of her sweatshirt, and a rip just above the knee of her faded jeans offered a tantalizing glimpse of her thigh.

"Adam." Her eyebrows lifted in surprise. "Were you just talking to someone?"

"A woman heading west up the street. Short gray hair, about five feet five, red umbrella and boots."

"That sounds like Betty Randall. She's a widow who lives on a couple of acres, across the field behind us. She has lots of time on her hands and keeps an eye on the area, either by walking or driving around."

"Like a neighborhood watch."

"In a way. She's a bit of a gossip, but she's been sweet to William and me. What are you doing here?"

Hell if he knew. He scratched the back of his neck. "Figured I'd stop by and see how you're doing. You aren't baking right now, are you?"

"In this outfit?" She glanced down at herself and laughed. "When I work, I wear an apron and a hairnet. You don't want to see that. Although, while William is in kindergarten, I should be mixing ingredients for later. Instead, I'm trying to fix a small plumbing problem."

"Then it's a good thing I'm here."

"You know about plumbing?"

"I'm a firefighter. I know a lot of stuff. What's the problem?"

"The hot water faucet in the tub upstairs is leaking, and I'm pretty sure the washer needs to be replaced," she said. "The trouble is, I can't get the old one off, to take it to the hardware store and get the right size. I've been trying to remove it for a while now."

"I can do that."

She opened the door wider. Adam wiped his feet on the welcome mat and stepped into a gleaming slate entry. Beyond it, he could see gleaming hardwood floors and thick, oriental rugs that covered the living and dining rooms. He noted Sam's fuzzy pink socks. "Should I take my shoes off?"

"You're fine."

He followed her into a living room of expensive-looking armchairs and a big couch, oriented toward a stone fireplace. The plastic crate piled with toys sitting against one wall looked like a poor relative.

The house had a solid, warm feel. That and the faint aroma of cinnamon, coffee, and home cooking made it feel like what he'd always imagined a real home should be. His mom had never been much of a cook, and the drafty place where his family had lived when he was a kid had smelled of canned food, frozen dinners, and cigarettes.

"Nice place," he said.

"I know. I'm so lucky I saw Miss Marks's ad for a house sitter before anyone else did. She has a big, dream kitchen that's been updated and remodeled. Perfect for what I do. I get to stay here through mid-June." She hugged herself and smiled, as if she couldn't believe her good fortune.

"Then what?"

"If my business continues to do well, by then I should have enough saved for first and last months' rent on a nice little house, with enough left over to rent commercial kitchen space."

"Why would you want a commercial space?"

"For licensing purposes, I really should do my baking in a commercial kitchen. Plus, a separate space would be easier to keep clean."

"Heck, with your baking talent, you could open your own bakery."

"That's my dream. Someday."

"People will line up around the block."

"That's another dream of mine."

The mischievous slant of her mouth pulled him in, and he was sorely tempted to kiss her. *Nope, not gonna happen.* He started to shove his hands into his pockets, but the bandage he'd slipped on after leaving his pop's earlier and his still-sore wrist stopped him.

"Show me that faucet," he said.

"Right this way."

She led him up a carpeted staircase not quite wide enough for them to walk side by side. Lagging a few steps behind, he enjoyed the view. The sway of her hips, her sweet rear end. And those socks.... Why he thought they were sexy was anyone's guess.

Upstairs, they passed several bedrooms. No doubt, the one with the single bed, the toys, and kids' books belonged to William. Another looked unused. The third room with its neatly-made queen-size bed and the woman's ankle boots on the floor—this was where Sam slept.

Adam's body liked knowing that and started to jump to life. Not where he wanted to go, and he turned his thoughts to the task at hand.

She led him into the bathroom and pointed at the faucets on the claw-foot tub. "That's where the leak is. I already turned off the water in here."

He was impressed she'd known to do that. Various tools were spread on an old towel on the blue-and-white tile floor. Adam hunkered down beside the tub. "Hand me that adjustable wrench."

Sam did, then leaned against the wall to watch. "Do you miss not staying overnight at the station?" she asked as he fit the wrench to the faucet.

"We each have our own quarters, so not the sleeping per se. I sure miss the noise, though. After nine years of spending a chunk of each week with a bunch of guys, I've gotten used to it."

Sam yawned. "When I fall asleep, I can sleep through anything. But that's because I'm up at three to bake."

"Ugh," Adam said. "That can happen at the station, too, if we get a call. Some nights, we never get to bed at all." He handed Sam the wrench and pulled out the washer. "There. It's off."

"Finally. Now I can go to the hardware store and buy the right one."

"This looks like your standard-issue washer," Adam said. "I'll bet Lucy has a couple extras stashed someplace."

"If she does, I have no idea where. And I don't want to call and bother her with this."

"Does she have a catch-all drawer or a place where she keeps nails?"

"Hmmm." Sam's brow wrinkled in thought. "Maybe in the basement? That's where I found these tools."

"I'll check."

"Are you sure? Don't you have better things to do?"

Adam thought about the management book at his place, waiting for him to crack open. He was in no hurry to get back. "I'm good."

"While you look for a washer, I'll make a fresh pot

of coffee. Do you like your cinnamon rolls at room temp or warmed up?"

"Warm," he said, salivating at the thought.

Downstairs, Sam led him to the kitchen, a roomy space with double ovens and a gleaming tile floor. She opened the door to the basement and flicked on the light.

"To the left of the washer and dryer, there's a board with tools hanging on it," she said.

He thudded down the worn, wooden steps into a standard basement. No remodeling down here. On the way to the tool board, he passed a clothes line, where a couple of lacy bras and panties hung. He couldn't help wondering what Sam wore under that old sweatshirt. Shaking his head at his wayward thoughts, he located the tool drawer beneath the tool board. There, he found a packet of washers. He and Sam returned to the second floor, and in no time, the new washer was in place. He turned on the water supply again, and then Sam tested the faucet. After a few spurts and gurgles, hot water gushed out. She shut it off. Not a drip in sight.

"Thanks, Adam," she said, beaming at him. "You saved the day. Come downstairs and get your reward."

Ridiculously pleased to have put that smile on her face, he washed up. They sat down at a kitchen table big enough for six, where the promised coffee and oven-warmed cinnamon rolls waited. Licking his lips, Adam helped himself to both.

While he devoured a couple of rolls, he noted a crayon drawing hanging on the fridge. At the bottom, shaky letters spelled out William's name. "Your son likes to draw," he commented, nodding at a corkboard near the back door, on which several other pictures were tacked. "Are those horses?"

Sam nodded. "I told you about Betty Randall, our widowed neighbor with the red boots and umbrella. Her kids have grown up and moved away, and she misses her grandchildren. I think that's why she dotes on William. Occasionally, when I'm in a pinch, she even babysits. William likes her, and he adores the two old horses that live in her barn."

"The ones in the drawing," Adam guessed.

"That's right. He's always begging to visit them. In fact, I promised we'd go over there this afternoon, after William's nap. If he naps. He claims he's ready to give them up, but I'm not. I use the time to work...or I used to." She laughed. "These days, bribery is the only way I can get him to lie down."

Her laugh was contagious. Adam grinned. "He's a busy little guy."

"Don't I know it. He keeps me on my toes."

Adam could tell she was a terrific mom.

"I think he may have artistic talent," Sam said.

He nodded. "Does he get that from you or his father?" he asked, wanting to know about Sam's ex.

Her sudden, deep frown made him wish he hadn't asked.

"A distant cousin of my dad was a cartoonist, so maybe from him. But Jeff?" She wrinkled her nose in distaste. "He doesn't have an artistic bone in his body."

"You don't like your ex much," Adam guessed.

"Why should I? He hasn't given his son the time of day since he walked out on us almost three years ago."

"That sucks." Adam shook his head and wondered how any man could walk away from this woman and her kid. A woman he'd started to like way more than was smart. "If you don't mind my asking, what happened?"

"I don't mind. Things between us had gotten a

little tense and awkward. I should have known something was off, but between William and my apprenticeship at the local bakery, I was so busy I didn't even realize he'd fallen in love with someone else."

"Ouch."

"It was a big shock. The second our divorce became final, Jeff and Kayla got married. Fun times, for sure." She snorted. "As difficult as the whole thing was for me, at least my adult brain could deal with it," she went on. "But at barely two, William couldn't possibly understand. He really missed his dad. It took over six months before he stopped asking for him. I will never forgive Jeff for that."

Sam was a small woman, didn't quite reach Adam's armpit. But when she crossed her arms, compressed her lips and narrowed her eyes, she reminded him of a mama bear, determined to protect her cub at all costs. Angry and protective. Irresistible.

He wanted to lean across the table, cup her indignant face in his hands, and kiss her until she forgot her ex and the grief he'd caused. But that meant trouble he didn't want or need.

He took a long pull of his coffee. "Jeff sounds like a real jerk."

"He is."

"I got married once, when I was eighteen."

"So young."

"Too young. Neither of us was ready to settle down." Understatement of the year. "Looking back, we both confused teenage lust with love."

As soon as the thrill of sex anytime, day or night, had worn off, the marriage had quickly soured. Adam had dealt with his problems the same way his father had—drinking and staying out late. He and Fawn had argued a lot about that. One night after an especially bad fight, he'd headed for a bar and stayed until closing. Then he'd gone home with a woman he barely knew. Two weeks later, Fawn had filed for divorce.

By then, their marriage had been over for months. Still, Adam blamed himself. He wasn't proud he'd cheated on her. Since then, he'd cleaned up his act. Now, he rarely drank more than two beers in an evening, and when he dated a woman, he didn't fool around with anyone else.

None of that changed the fact he sucked at relationships.

"Your girlfriend must be happy you're home every night for a change," Sam said. "I'll bet she misses you during those forty-eight-hour shifts."

"I'm not dating anyone right now." It'd been months, which explained why he was jonesing for sex and wanting so bad to kiss Sam.

Time to out of here. He cleared his throat. "I should get going. Thanks for the coffee and cinnamon rolls."

"Thanks for fixing the faucet."

Adam helped her clear the table. At the door, she handed him his jacket.

Unable to stop himself, he removed the ridiculous clip holding Sam's bangs. His fingers lingered on her forehead, and he trailed them down her cheek. She had the softest skin.

She sucked in a startled breath, and he fully expected her to bat him away. Instead, she surprised him, her expression softening and warming, her lips relaxing into lush fullness.

Desire hit like a fist to the gut, and he forgot all about leaving. He wanted to taste her. Needed to. He grasped her forearms and pulled her up nice and close.

"What are you doing?" she asked, the question belied by the flare of heat in her eyes.

"What I wanted to do since I knocked on your door. This." He brushed his mouth over hers, teasing and testing.

For one paralyzing moment, she just stood there without responding. He expected her to pull away, but instead, her eyelids drifted shut. With a soft sigh, she wrapped her arms around his shoulders and returned the kiss. Sweet and eager, better than he'd imagined in any late-night fantasy. And lately, he'd had more than a few of those.

He angled his head and touched the seam between her lips with his tongue. They parted and she welcomed him. She tasted of coffee and cinnamon roll and something underneath that was hers alone.

He was hard with need and ready to haul her upstairs to that bed of hers, get naked and sink into her heat, when she pushed her palms against his chest and broke the kiss.

"Stop it, Adam."

As winded as if he'd sprinted up three-story building during a fire, he released her.

Her cheeks were flushed, her pupils dilated and that mouth of hers…. Pink and a little swollen. Sweet jeezus.

Adam swallowed. "I, uh, if I stepped out of line, I apologize."

He waited for Sam to comment. Instead, she gave a dazed nod. He touched her cheek again. "I'll see you later."

Aroused and aching, he walked out, shaking his head at what he'd started. He ought to be sorry, but all he could think about was coming back for more.

As SOON AS the door shut behind Adam, Samantha sank against it—as if the hard wood could cool her down. She hadn't been held by a man since her marriage had started crumbling months before Jeff walked out, and except for an occasional peck on the cheek from William or her dad, she hadn't been kissed. Not like this, with a thoroughness and hunger deeper than anything she'd experienced.

Remembering, she went all tingly and antsy and wanting more, and knew she'd made a big mistake.

She glanced at the clock, surprised to see how late it was. There was no time to reflect on what had happened, let alone change out of her grubby clothes. She had to leave right now, or she'd be late picking up William. Samantha snatched her purse from the hook near the door and hurried out.

"Where are the carrots I gave you?" Samantha asked as she and William cut across the field behind the house. This morning's sleet had melted away. The clouds had lifted, and the weak winter sun glinting off the trees made for a pretty walk.

"Right here." William stopped mid-step. Tongue peeking from the corner of his mouth, he pulled several carrots from the pockets of his parka.

Despite Samantha's attempts at bribery—a nap in exchange for the visit—her son was too keyed about seeing Betty, whom he called Mrs. Randall, and Gordy and Cocoa, the two bay geldings stabled in her barn, to even consider a rest. So here they were, tromping across the field shortly after lunch.

William shoved the horse treats back into his pockets, and they continued forward.

"Do you think Gordy and Cocoa will be glad to see me?" he asked, his expression both solemn and hopeful.

After nearly six months of weekly visits, he was still insecure, even about the friendship of the big animals. Just one of the lingering side-effects caused by his father's desertion.

Samantha's heart broke a little, and for the thousandth time she wanted to strangle Jeff for his callousness. "They'll be thrilled to see you, sweetie."

As if to attest to her words, the horses whinnied in the distance. "Did you hear that?" She smiled. "They know you're on the way."

"Here I come, guys!" William hollered.

He started to run, mud sucking at his boots. Picking her way around puddles, Samantha followed more slowly. By the time she reached her neighbor's house, William had clomped across the porch to ring the doorbell.

Betty answered with a broad smile. "Hello there, William. It's good to see you, Samantha. I walked past your house earlier and saw that you had a visitor."

She knew the grisly details about Jeff and why Samantha had moved to Guff's Lake to start fresh. Not one to hold back her opinion, she'd been pushing Samantha to start dating again.

Her speculative look made Samantha nervous. She didn't want any questions or gossip about Adam's visit. "A minor plumbing problem," she explained.

"Ah." Betty engulfed William in a warm hug that caused her son to giggle. Then she gestured them inside. Samantha reminded William to wipe his feet on the mat first.

As soon as William stepped through the door, he showed the older woman the carrots.

She nodded. "Cocoa and Gordy will be very happy for those."

"We brought you something, too." Samantha handed her neighbor a sack containing the scone and muffin she'd set aside from that day's orders.

"I hoped you would." Eyes twinkling, Betty rubbed her ample stomach. "How about a cup of coffee, Samantha? I have hot cocoa for you, William. The kind you like, with the mini-marshmallows."

Usually, her son would have raced to the kitchen in excitement. Today he hesitated. "But I want to see the horses."

Samantha gave an apologetic shrug. "Maybe after?" she asked the older woman.

"Of course. Let me grab my coat and we'll go on out."

The weathered barn stood roughly thirty feet beyond the house and was just big enough for two stalls, a shelf for supplies, and a half-dozen bales of hay.

With gentle coaching from Betty, William took turns with the bays, blowing gently on one gelding's nostrils before offering a carrot, then the other. Enjoying a few minutes of rare R and R, Samantha perched on a giant hay bale, leaned back against the raw plank wall, and let her thoughts wander.

Here in the stable with her son and her neighbor, she could almost forget about this morning with Adam.

Almost, but not quite. Absently, she touched her lips and recalled the corded strength of his arms, holding her against his broad, solid chest. His mouth, hungry on hers. His arousal....

Who was she kidding? She couldn't forget a second of Adam's bone-melting kisses.

For three years, she'd been indifferent to masculine attention and uninterested in sex. But now, Adam had gone and changed everything.

She wanted him to kiss her again and make her world spin. To taste his desire, press up close to his hard body.

She had to admit she wanted more than kisses. A lot more.

The dangerous thought scared her. She couldn't allow herself to want Adam, and not just to protect herself. Jeff's neglect had deeply wounded William. He didn't need to get close to another man, only to be hurt again.

For both her and her son's sakes, she needed to steer clear of Adam.

That shouldn't be a problem, as they didn't exactly hang out in the same social circles. Samantha didn't even have a social circle. Friends, yes, but not much time for socializing.

She doubted she would see Adam again.

"Mom?" William frowned.

"What, sweetie?"

"I said, can we invite Adam over for dinner?"

The question caught her by surprise. Her son hadn't mentioned the man since their trip to the fire station earlier in the week.

"Who's Adam?" Betty asked, raising her eyebrows.

"A super-duper cool firefighter," William replied. "He put out the fire in Rosemary's kitchen, and he showed me around the station, and I got to sit in the fire truck and look in the ambulance, and I had an awesome time." His chest puffed out.

Betty gave a canny smile. "That does sound super-duper cool."

"It's not what you think," Samantha hastened to explain.

"What I think is, you're young and single, and your son could use some male influence."

"What's male ifflence?" William asked.

"It means grownup men who are friends,"

Samantha explained, giving her neighbor a pointed, stay-out-of-this look.

"Adam is a man and a grownup," William said. "And I want him to be my friend."

"I'm sure he'd like that, but he's very busy. Now, I need to speak privately with Mrs. Randall. Then we should get back so I can do some prep work for tonight's baking. Will you wait for me here?"

"But what about my cocoa?"

"Why don't we save that until next time? We'll be in the kitchen. If you decide to leave the barn, come straight there, all right?"

William nodded and then moved closer to the stalls.

As outspoken and opinionated as Betty Randall tended to be, she was equally open to hearing what others had to say. As soon as Samantha could speak without her son hearing, she shared her thoughts.

"When William is in the room, please don't talk about him in the third person," she said, remembering times when her parents had spoken about her when she'd been right there. "I don't want him feeling like he's invisible."

"I should have thought of that. From now on, when William and I are in the same room, I'll address any comments about him directly to him."

Relieved the woman understood, Samantha relaxed. "Thanks. Now I have a question. What exactly did you mean about male influence?"

"Only that William could do with a male role model in his life."

"He has a good one. My dad. Once or twice a month, they talk on the phone."

"But how often do they see each other?"

Betty knew the answer to her own question—not since Samantha and William had left Enterprise. Over the Christmas holiday, Samantha hadn't been up for the ten-plus-hour drive or crossing the snowy Siskiyou Mountains to visit Enterprise. She couldn't afford airfare, either, let alone the time away from her baking.

Her parents had felt the same way about traveling to Guff's Lake. It was unlikely William would see them again until summer.

"I rest my case. Bringing another man into William's life can't hurt."

Oh, but it could.

"You worry because his father walked out," Betty said. "That doesn't mean all men would."

"I can't take that chance."

"I understand, dear. Are you sure you don't want coffee? It's still hot."

"I wish I could, but I really have to get home and do some work...if I can pry William away from you and the horses."

Betty chuckled. "I'll make myself scarce, then. Shut the barn door when you leave. And come back soon."

"We will."

After hugging her neighbor, Samantha returned to the barn to collect William.

As she'd expected, he put up a fuss about leaving.

"Mrs. Randall has things to do, and so do I, remember?" she said.

He wore that stubborn, clamped-jaw look, so Samantha tried a different tack, one sure to appeal to his growing sense of independence. "I'll bet you're big enough to close the barn door by yourself today," she said. "Then we have to leave."

He brightened right up. "Okay."

While he struggled with the heavy latch, his tongue poked out.

"Need some help?" Samantha asked, ready to step in.

"No." After much grunting and effort, he succeeded. "I did it!" he crowed, looking very proud. "High-five me, Mom."

Samantha did. Then they headed for home.

On the walk back, her son brought up Adam again. "Please, Mom, can we invite him over for dinner? He'll like our house."

He had no idea Adam had seen the house this morning. He'd made Samantha want things she wasn't ready for, and she wasn't about to invite him back.

Even more important, she didn't want William getting attached. "Adam works long hours at the station," she explained. "I doubt he has the time for dinner with us."

"But, Mom, he likes us. I could tell. He'll come, I know it."

"Maybe sometime," she hedged. "But not right now. Adam and I are both too busy."

Her son heaved a dramatic sigh and dragged his boots across the muddy ground.

"Guess what happens on Friday?" Samantha said, changing the subject. "I get paid. You know what that means."

"Saturday hotdogs and curly fries at The Rogue!" Dragging feet forgotten, William pumped his fist.

During the rest of the walk home, he chattered about his friends Douglas and Harper, and how they'd practiced their ninja moves at recess. He didn't mention the firefighter again.

Relieved, Samantha gave her brow a mental swipe.

With any luck, in a day or two, William would forget all about Adam Healey. And so would she.

WHEN POSSIBLE, Adam and his crewmates played poker on Friday nights. The game moved from house to house. Anyone from the station was welcome, and you never knew who might show up.

Adam had hosted a month ago. Tonight's game was at Rob's. Besides Adam, Nate and Ethan showed up, rounding out the table.

Adam puffed on a cigar and laid down his cards. "Three queens."

The other players tossed in their hands and swore. As tight as they were and as much as they trusted each other to have each other's backs, not one of them enjoyed losing.

Nate shuffled. "How's Richard doing?" he asked Adam as he dealt new cards.

Everyone knew about Adam's father. Even though he'd retired from his job as captain long before any of them had started working at the station, they'd all met him once or twice.

"He's doing okay," Adam said. "As sick as he is, he's still the same SOB as ever."

This hand wasn't as good as the previous one, but not bad. With four of the five cards in the same suit, he could end up with a flush. He discarded the odd card out. "Hit me, Nate. One card."

Nate dealt him a replacement in the suit Adam needed, giving him the flush. Stifling a triumphant grin, he maintained a somber expression and tossed in a couple of chips. "I'll be at his place tomorrow, busting my chops to clean his gutters, but you know he'll give me hell for it."

"He's damn lucky to have your help." Rob studied his cards then tossed his two chips into the kitty.

Adam shrugged. "Someone has to keep the place up for him."

Ethan threw down his cards. "I fold," he said around the cigar clamped between his teeth. "If you're in good-enough shape to climb up to the roof and clean gutters, you're probably ready for regular duty."

"I see the doctor Monday." With his uninjured hand, Adam crossed his fingers and held them up.

His flush won him the pot again.

"The poker god is with you tonight," Ethan said. He yawned and stretched. "I'm tired of losing and ready to pack it in. Got a gig tomorrow night, and I'll be up till all hours." He pantomimed playing his sax.

When not on duty, he and the other three members of Mello, the jazz band he'd founded, worked steadily.

"Got a hot date afterward?" Rob asked.

"Not yet, but I will." Ethan winked. The combination of firefighting and local jazz star made him a primo babe magnet, and he knew it. "We're playing at Lucky Joe's, and you know what that means—plenty of single women."

Saturday nights, the popular bar on the west side of town featured live music and always played to a packed house.

Although Adam had heard Mello perform numerous times, he seriously considered spending Saturday night at Lucky Joe's. Hell, he needed to do something. If he met a willing woman, all the better.

On the heels of the thought, he wondered if Sam liked jazz.

Forget that. After he'd cooled off the other day and come to his senses, he'd decided to steer clear of her and her son. He wanted her, but he didn't want the trouble that getting tangled up with her would surely cause.

So why did he keep fantasizing about her?

"What's with the frown?" Nate asked as they put away the cards and chips. "You trounced us good tonight and pocketed ten whole bucks."

Adam blew on his nails then polished them on his shirt. "I'm number one."

"This week," Ethan said. "Cocky bastard."

"That I am. Where's the action next week?" Adam asked as he shrugged into his bomber jacket.

Rob consulted his smart phone for the poker schedule set up by the station's tech genius, Owen. "At Rafe's place."

They walked out together.

Adam warmed up the 4Runner then headed toward home. It was a cold, clear evening, with stars and a bright, three-quarter moon. A night made for crawling under the covers with a warm, willing woman. Adam fantasized Sam, naked and hungry under him. His jeans fly grew uncomfortably tight.

"Damn," he muttered. He was not going to think about her.

He popped a Keb'Mo' album into the CD player and cranked up the volume nice and loud. The bluesy tunes drowned out his thoughts. He was singing along with "Dirty Low Down and Bad" when he realized he'd taken a detour.

Instead of driving toward his place, he tooled down Sam's street. How had that happened?

Snickering at himself, he slowed to a crawl and rolled past the house. Not a single light on that he could see. Which made sense, as she had to get up super early to bake and make deliveries.

He wasn't sure if he was relieved or disappointed, but ending up here settled any doubts about his plans for tomorrow night.

He would definitely go to Lucky Joe's.

6

As promised, around noon Samantha pulled into the parking lot of The Rogue, the Denney's-style restaurant William loved.

The lot was packed, normal for lunchtime on a Saturday. As she searched for a parking space, a fire-color 4Runner caught her eye. As far as she knew, only one person in town drove a car that color, and the license plate number "1-Adam" and its Professional Firefighter tag erased any doubts that the car was his.

Adam was here.

Samantha's stomach fluttered, as it did every time she thought about him. Which was a lot, no matter how hard she tried to forget.

Seeing him wouldn't help, and she almost turned the car around and left. But she'd promised William. Maybe they'd run an errand and come back later.

"I'm so hungry I'm going to order two cheesy hotdogs and curly fries with ketchup. And chocolate milk," he announced, almost as if he sensed her reluctance to go inside. "What are you going to eat, Mom?"

She was no coward, Samantha told herself. She would say hello, just as she would anyone, then find a table for her and William, where they would enjoy their lunch. "A patty melt and sweet potato fries. I see a parking slot at the end of this row."

Moments later, she let William out of the car. Fearing he would bolt across the busy lot, she reached for his hand. "Let's check for moving cars," she reminded him.

After a quick glance around, her eager son tugged her forward. Keeping a wary eye out for traffic, she let him pull her along at a fast clip. The second he reached the entrance to the restaurant, he released her hand and attempted to open the heavy door by himself. He couldn't manage it. Samantha helped him, and they stepped inside.

The large restaurant was crowded and noisy, with servers rushing here and there. Yet she found Adam right away. He sat at a table for two in front of a side window, hunched over what looked like a textbook.

His broad shoulders strained his unbuttoned flannel shirt. The grey T-shirt underneath hugged his chest and flat belly. And those biceps... He was the best-looking man in the room.

"I see Adam!" William pointed at him.

By the time Samantha jerked her head from the clouds, her son had raced forward, shouting Adam's name.

Kids at nearby tables gaped at him, and the adults with them looked equally curious. Recognizing a few familiar faces, Samantha smiled and shrugged as she chased after her son.

Wearing a friendly expression, Adam shut the book. "Hey there, sport."

Winter sunlight streamed through the window, making his eyes look especially blue. Samantha heard the collective sighs of admiration from the women in the room.

"Hey, Sam."

His grin amped up to killer level, wreaking serious havoc inside her. Her lips tingled, her nipples tightened, and her whole body yearned for him. Somehow, she managed an easy smile. "Hi, Adam. I didn't expect to find you here."

"My pop lives a couple miles away, and by the time I left his place earlier this morning, I needed food." He gestured at the empty plates he'd pushed aside. "By the way, my pop is crazy about your treats, especially the blueberry muffins."

Oblivious of the electricity arcing between her and Adam—or maybe because he sensed it, but didn't understand it—William began to chatter. "We got paid, and today we get to eat lunch here! Mom says I can have chocolate milk and cheesy hotdogs and curly fries. With ketchup."

Adam looked amused. "Ketchup, too?"

"Uh-huh. What did you have?"

"A spicy chicken melt and chips."

William made a face. "I don't like spicy food."

"You're studying," Samantha said. When he nodded, she went on. "We'll leave you to it, then. Come on, William, let's find a table."

She started to turn away from the man who made her long for things she couldn't afford to want, but William dug in his heels and tugged on her coat.

"Wait, Mom! We can ask Adam right now."

He would mention his dinner idea. "This isn't a good time, William. Adam needs to study."

Adam looked curious. "Ask me what?"

"To come to our house for dinner tonight!" William boomed.

The room grew noticeably quieter as nosey customers waited for Adam's answer. Samantha's face burned, and she knew she was blushing.

WILLIAM'S very loud question had drawn interest from everyone within hearing distance, but Sam's suddenly scarlet cheeks held Adam's attention. He couldn't help but remember her flushed skin after the kisses that had knocked his socks off.

What the hell was everyone staring at? He recognized some people but none well enough to know their names. He raised his eyebrows, as if to say, "Butt out," and they returned to their meals.

If Sam cooked half as well as she baked, dinner would be delicious. His unwanted lust for her made accepting the invitation a bad idea. But with William jumping up and down with excitement.... Adam hated to deflate the kid's balloon.

Having suffered his own disappointment at his father's earlier today, he knew how rotten that felt. Richard had been in rare form this morning, especially when Adam arrived empty-handed. After a restless night, he'd been in no mood to stop at Rosemary's and pick up a muffin.

Big mistake. The old man had growled at him to go home and not to come back—ever—empty-handed.

Was that all he meant to his father—the bearer of treats?

Adam had had half a mind to do as Richard asked, leave and stay away. Instead, he'd sucked it up and cleaned the gutters as planned.

Not a word of thanks or a trace of a smile, just an-

other scowl, deafening volume on the tube and a muttered good-bye. What had Adam expected?

He'd left with a scowl of his own, more determined
than ever to ace the written exam for lieutenant, get
the promotion, and earn the old man's respect.

Eager to grab lunch and hit the books, he'd chosen
The Rogue, where he wouldn't likely run into friends.

"Can you, Adam?" William prodded.

"Uh...." Not sure how to respond to the invitation,
he looked to Sam for help.

"William spoke out of turn, Adam."

The boy raised his hand. She frowned. "Why is
your hand up?"

"I'm waiting for my turn."

Adam chuckled. "Go ahead, William."

"Can you please come over tonight? Please, please,
please?"

Adam could see Sam was just as torn about dinner
together. "Do you want me there?" he asked her.

She brushed at something on her coat sleeve before she replied. "The thing is, we're having a very
simple meal that includes chicken, and you had a
chicken sandwich for lunch. And it is Saturday night.
I'm sure you have something else to do."

Talk about excuses. She didn't want him to come.

He was off the hook. Great. Still, it stung. Go
figure.

He opened his mouth to explain that yeah, he did
have plans and wouldn't be able to make it, when she
bit her lip and gave him a pleading look. "On the other
hand, it would mean a lot to William if you joined us."

The about-face surprised Adam, but he understood that dinner tonight wasn't about him and Sam.
This was about pleasing her son. Adam silently ap-

plauded her for caring so much about his happiness. The little guy didn't realize how lucky he was.

Having heard Nate and Mello at Lucky Joe's several times, Adam knew they wouldn't start their gig until later in the evening. He could indulge the kid and still see the band. He nodded. "Sure, I can make dinner."

As for his crazy attraction to Sam, as long as he focused on William instead of her, there was nothing to worry about.

"Awesome!"

The boy's toothy smile made Adam feel ten feet tall. "What time?"

"William's bedtime is seven-thirty, and my day started way before dawn, so it's going to be an early night for us. We'll sit down at six."

"Eighteen-hundred hours. That's when we eat at the station."

"No...six o'clock," William corrected.

Adam nodded. "They're one and the same, only we use military time at the station."

"What's military time?"

Adam explained in simple terms, until William seemed satisfied. Knowing it would be an early night for Sam and the boy suited him just fine. "What can I bring?"

"Not a thing. I have everything we need. You're sure you don't mind chicken?"

"Nope. It's one of my favorites. Why don't I bring a bottle of wine? Red or white?"

"Either. I drink both."

"Will you bring your firefighter hat?" William asked.

"You like the hat, huh?"

The boy gave an enthusiastic nod that had Adam

chuckling again. After Richard's sour reception this morning, the lightheartedness felt good. "Sure, I'll bring it."

Adam's server, a twenty-something woman, brought the coffee pot over and refilled his mug with a flirty smile. She was cute, but he hadn't been interested in her when she'd flirted earlier, and for damn sure he wasn't now.

"I should feed my son, and you need to study." Sam placed her hands on William's narrow shoulders and propelled him toward a booth on the other side of the room.

Adam reached for his textbook but ignored it to stare at Sam and her tight jeans tucked into flat-sole knee boots. Bending forward slightly, she guided William. Her unbuttoned coat hid the curve of her sweet behind.

Between the boots and the bulky coat, she looked shapeless. All the same, she turned him on. He got hard, like when he'd been a hormone-crazed teen.

Muttering and grateful for the table hiding his lap, he questioned himself for agreeing to the dinner. Even if he was doing it for William.

And okay, he also wanted to be there.

Refusing to think beyond that, he went back to studying.

7

As soon as Samantha slid the casserole into the oven and made the salad, she headed for the living room. She found William on the floor, pushing his toy racecars around the oriental rug. Firelight from the crackling fire cast golden light across his adorable face.

"When will Adam get here?" he asked for what had to be the hundredth time.

He was so excited about this. Samantha refused to even wonder at her own anticipation. Tonight was about William, she reminded herself. Aside from little things, he didn't ask for much. In his five years of life, he'd already suffered far too much disappointment. If eating dinner with Adam made him happy, then great.

Provided Adam actually showed up.

Before Jeff, such a thought would never have occurred to her. Now, the possibility filled her mind, making her anxious and cold inside.

William's brow furrowed. "Do you have a tummy ache?"

Catching herself hugging her waist and frowning, Samantha dropped her hands to her sides. "I'm fine," she replied, smiling.

Adam wouldn't let her son down. He said he'd be here, and he would. "Why don't you wash up and help me set the table? We're eating in the dining room tonight."

William nodded and jumped up.

Despite reassuring herself, apprehension stayed with her. As her son arranged napkins and silverware on the good placemats, she worried all over again Adam wouldn't show up.

Then the old doorbell chimed. Feeling silly for doubting him, she drew in a normal breath for the first time in hours.

"He's here!" William raced out of the dining room and headed for the entry, Samantha close behind him.

"Do not unlock the door until I say so," she ordered.

In Guff's Lake, people tended to leave their doors unlocked, but she didn't feel comfortable doing that. Not with a young son to keep an eye on, at a house she was supposed to be taking care of.

He pulled a long face. "But, Mom, we know it's Adam."

"Let's check anyway. He won't mind." She dragged over the child's wooden stepstool she'd bought at Second Hand Rose, one of her favorite places to shop.

William climbed up and framed the peephole between his hands. "I see him!" He clambered down again.

"That didn't take any time at all, did it?" Samantha moved the step stool aside. "Go ahead and let him in, William."

Her son unlocked the deadbolt then, grunting with effort, pulled the heavy door open. "Hi, Adam!"

"Hey, sport."

Clasping his firefighter hat under his arm and a

large paper bag with handles, he wiped his feet on the welcome mat and stepped inside.

The entry seemed smaller with him filling it. He shrugged out of his bomber jacket, and Samantha hung it in the closet. Tonight, he'd dressed up in wool pants, tassel loafers, and a long-sleeve, pressed shirt that emphasized his broad shoulders. Samantha's wayward heart lifted on a sigh. Such a handsome man. But then, he looked just as great in jeans and a flannel shirt.

"Nice fire," he said, nodding at the hearth.

"I helped Mom bring in the logs," William announced proudly.

Adam gave an approving nod. "It's always good to help your mom." He sniffed the air and rubbed his hands together. "Sure smells good in here. I'm hungry."

Samantha laughed, and the last of her anxiety faded away. "Dinner's almost ready."

"We're having chicken casserole and salad and coconut cream pie for dessert," William said. "How come you aren't wearing your hat?"

"I don't wear it unless I'm fighting a fire."

"Why not?"

"Because it's part of my turnout gear. Remember what that is? The protective clothing I wear when I'm called to a fire."

While William seemed to consider this, Adam donned the hat. "How's that?"

"Good." Her son nodded somberly. "There's no fire to fight here. You can take it off now."

Adam did. "Where should I put this, Sam?"

"How about in the living room?"

He placed it on the floor, in the corner near the couch.

William's attention had strayed to the sack Adam had left in the entry. "What did you bring me?" he asked.

"It's not polite to ask," Samantha scolded, but her own curiosity got the better of her. "That's a pretty big bag for one little bottle of wine."

Adam's mouth quirked. "There might be a few other things in here." He scooped it up and pulled out a firefighter hat just the right size for William. "This is for you, sport."

"Thanks!" William beamed. "Wait till Douglas and Harper see this. Can I bring it to school, for show and tell, Mom?"

"Of course." Samantha's heart melted. "This is so sweet, Adam."

The flush that climbed his neck and face charmed her.

Looking very somber, William hugged the hat to his chest.

"Aren't you going to try it on?" Adam asked.

"I can't. We don't have a fire, except in the fireplace."

"That rule is only for real firefighters," Adam said. "It's okay to wear yours anytime."

Her son's face lit up. He placed the hat his head and laughed. "I'm a firefighter! Uh-oh, there's a fire in the other room!" Wielding an imaginary fire hose and making water-spraying noises, he raced through the dining room, into the kitchen and back.

"I got you something, too." Adam brought out a potted plant. "This is a philodendron. It likes light, but not direct sunlight, and should be watered once a week."

No man had ever given her a plant before. Samantha was touched. Tonight, Adam was doing everything right. She felt warm and happy—way too much of each—and knew she was in trouble. If only they'd eaten and William was ready for bed. Then Adam would leave and she could pull herself together. Unfortunately, dinner wasn't ready yet, and William was nowhere near ready to go to sleep.

"It's pretty," she said, fixing her attention on the leafy plant instead of the man who made her heart race. "I had no idea you were into plants."

"I'm not. My mom has one, and she seems to like it."

He hadn't mentioned his mother before. "Does she live in town?"

He shook his head. "She and her husband live in Carmel. They own a carpet cleaning business there."

"Too bad they aren't in Guff's Lake. These carpets are going to need a thorough cleaning before Lucy comes back."

By then, the entire house would need a good scrubbing. Nothing to worry about now. Tonight was all about the gorgeous man standing in Samantha's living room. He smelled of fresh air, spicy aftershave, and man, and she had a crazy urge to press up close and inhale that scent. She was definitely in trouble.

Space, she needed space so she could talk some sense into herself. She set the plant on the end table beside the couch. "Make yourself comfortable while I toss the salad. Shall I open this wine?"

"Let me."

Instead of sitting, Adam grabbed the bottle and moved beside her. So much for space.

In the kitchen, she handed him the corkscrew and then pulled two wineglasses from the cabinet.

While he worked at the cork, she dressed the salad. "Does that bother your wrist?" she asked.

"Not much. When I remember to wear the bandage, it helps."

"You're barely limping anymore," she noted. "What does the doctor say about going back to work?"

"I'll find out at my checkup Monday. Cross your fingers."

"I will. Did you get your studying done?"

"For now. I should've studied last night, too, but I played poker with some of the guys from the station instead. I won the whole kitty. Ten bucks."

"Wow, that's a lot of money," she teased.

"Enough for coffee and a couple of your scones."

"At least you're smart about what you spend it on."

The cork finally popped loose. Adam filled the glasses and passed her one.

"To you," he said, tipping his glass in salute.

The warmth she saw in his eyes only heightened her growing feelings. At The Rogue she'd explained this would be an early night, but for her sake, she needed to say it again. Right now, while running through the house distracted William.

"Listen," she said in a voice too low for her son's ears. "I don't think—"

William raced into the kitchen. "Mom, can I wear my boots in the house?" Without waiting for her answer, he opened the back door off the kitchen and scooped his rubber boots from the stoop.

"I don't want those in here," Samantha said. "They're still muddy from when we brought in the wood this afternoon."

"But firefighters wear boots. And look, the mud is dry now." William held them up to show her.

"They're still dirty. They need to be washed before you put them on in the house."

"I'll wash them right now." A messy job that was sure to take awhile.

"It's almost dinner time," Samantha argued. "We'll clean them tomorrow."

William set his jaw. "I don't want to wait until tomorrow. I want to wash them now."

"We'll do it tomorrow," she repeated firmly.

"No!" He stamped his foot.

"Stop it, William. We have company."

"I don't care." Clutching the boots to his chest, he raised his chin in challenge.

"Better listen to your mom, sport," Adam said in a calm but commanding voice. "She's the boss."

"No, I'm the boss," William insisted.

"Nope. Your mom is."

His little chin slanted. "Is your mom the boss of you?"

"She was until I was a lot older than you are now. I did what she told me, even when I didn't want to. You have to do the same with your mom."

"Oh, all right." Grumbling, William returned the boots to the back step.

Adam had saved the day. Samantha gave him a grateful smile.

"Thank you, sweetie," she said when her son shut the door. "Dinner's almost ready. Go wash up."

"But I already did, before I set the table."

After glancing at Adam, he gave a meek nod and headed for the powder room.

"He used to obey me without question," she said. "But lately, it seems as if we're always butting heads."

The corner of Adam's mouth lifted. "My brother and I were the same way. Well, mostly me. A couple of licks from the old man's belt, and I changed my tune. For a while."

"Your father smacked you with a belt?" Samantha was horrified.

"Only when I made him extra mad. He mostly stuck with yelling."

"And your mom?"

"She buried her head in the sand. She didn't want to make things even worse."

"You mean he hit her, too?"

"Never, but he argued with her quite a bit." Adam shook his head. "The last time I saw that belt, I'd just turned eleven. By then, Marcus was fourteen, and bigger than Pop. When he came at me, my brother stepped between us and threatened to punch him one."

And Samantha had thought her parents were mean for taking away phone and TV privileges when she got into trouble. Her heart went out to Adam and his brother for the fear they must have faced.

"You're lucky to have a brother to stick up for you," she said.

"Had. He died."

"Oh, Adam. I'm so sorry."

"Yeah." His expression shuttered closed. "You started to say something earlier."

Apparently, he didn't want to talk about his brother. Samantha nodded. "Right. I just... I'm not looking to get involved. It's just not a good idea, and I don't want you to assume that what happened the other day will happen tonight. Because it won't." No matter how badly she wanted to kiss him.

"I'm right there with you on all counts, Sam. What I said came out of gratitude for the dinner invitation and because I think you're a great mom."

She'd misinterpreted his warmth. Adam wasn't interested in her, after all. Not in the way she was interested in him. A huge relief, really, because she'd meant what she said. Getting involved with him was risky at best, for both her and William.

And yet, a part of her was disappointed.

The timer pinged. "That little sound means dinner is ready." She shut off the oven. "William can't still be washing his hands. I'd better go see what he's up to. Have a seat in the dining room."

AFTER POLISHING off a large wedge of pie and draining the last of his coffee before the dancing fire, Adam leaned back in his armchair, stretched out his legs and patted his belly. "Dinner was great, but. this pie...the best ever." He grinned. "You could sell these along with your other bakery goods and make a mint."

In a matching chair, Sam looked equally content. "Someday, when I open my bakery. There's plenty left for seconds."

"I would, only there's no room at the inn."

She laughed. "Are you finished with your pie, William?"

The boy had settled down at last. Wearing his fire-fighter hat and sprawled on his belly on the oriental rug, he silently pushed a toy fire truck around.

He slid the brim of the hat back so he could look up at her. "Can I save it for tomorrow?"

"Sure."

Returning to his play, he yawned for the third time in a few minutes. Adam doubted he'd last much longer.

A comfortable silence fell over the room, both Adam and Sam staring at the fire. He'd done his part, had put a smile on the little guy's face tonight. And he'd kept his distance from Sam. Not so easy, even if neither of them wanted a repeat of the other day. Adam still desired her, and by the yearning expression he glimpsed on her face when she didn't know he was looking, the feeling was mutual.

Lucky thing they had a pint-size chaperone to make them behave. Because smart or dumb, Adam wanted a lot more than a replay.

For that reason, he ought to say good-night and walk away right now. But he was enjoying himself as he hadn't in a long time. As soon as William headed upstairs for the night, he would leave, he told himself.

Sam stretched lazily and broke the silence. "Sweetie, it's time to get ready for bed."

"Do I have to?" The kid looked to Adam instead of his mother.

"That's what your mom said, so yes," Adam replied.

Sam rewarded him with an appreciative smile. "You heard the man." When William still balked, she shrugged. "I guess I'll have to go up with you and help you get ready."

"No! I'm a big boy."

"Yes, you are. Put your PJs on, wash your face, and brush your teeth. Then pick out a bedtime story and bring it down here."

With his hat still on his head and his fire truck in his arms, William made his way up the stairs.

"He's a great kid," Adam said.

"Except when he tries to fight me. Why can't he be like me at his age?"

"What were you like?" he asked, wanting to know.

"Most of the time, I obeyed my parents. I don't have any siblings, so I got all their attention." She made a face. "They were experts at playing the guilt card. 'We're so disappointed in you' or 'We thought you were mature enough to make a better choice,'" she mimicked.

"An easy mark," Adam teased.

"Oh, I got away with a few things."

"Such as?"

"Silly stuff, like going into the girls' bathroom as soon as I got to school and trading the pants my mother made me wear for the tight jeans hidden in my backpack."

With her great legs and sweet curves, he could understand why her parents didn't want her wearing those jeans. She'd probably turned on every boy in high school.

"If I talked back to my parents, they grounded me," she added. "Once, they found out I snuck out with a boy instead of studying at a girlfriend's. I had to come directly from school to Everett's, the general store my parents still own and run, and either study or help out. At night, they allowed me to do homework and read books, but nothing else."

"You had it easy. By the time I started high school, my parents were too busy yelling at each other to notice what I did." He brushed something from his pants. "To notice me, period."

"And they divorced because of all the yelling?"

Adam shook his head. "Because Marcus died, and they didn't know how to handle it."

Unable to sit, he stood and moved to the fireplace. After opening the mesh curtain, he squatted in front of a brass pot filled with wood, pulled out a log, and added it to the fire. He closed the curtain but stayed put.

"That must have been a terrible time for them," Sam said. "If anything ever happened to William..."

She shuddered. "How old was your brother when he passed away?"

"Seventeen." Adam brushed his hands together, straightened, and returned to his chair. "He was in the middle of a crosswalk, moving with the walk light, when a taxi driver had a heart attack. He plowed right into Marcus."

A huge lump formed in Adam's throat. He never talked about this, not even with Rafe. He had no idea why he told Sam, and questioned whether he should continue. But now that he'd started, he needed to finish.

"I wanted to be just like him." To have the old man believe in him and look at him with love and admiration. "But I couldn't seem to do anything right, so I gave up and went the opposite direction. No matter how many stupid stunts I pulled, Marcus had my back. Then he was gone."

Adam had been lost and drowning in grief. He'd needed to talk about his feelings and get them out, but his parents had forbidden it. "We never mentioned what happened, and I learned real fast not to bring up the subject."

"That can't have been easy." Samantha clasped her hands in her lap. "How did you cope?"

Poorly. "I stayed away from home for long stretches of time, taking turns bunking with a couple of friends. I'm sure their parents got real tired of my face, but no one ever said anything. I guess they felt sorry for me."

His parents had never questioned where he'd gone or reacted when he returned. Almost as if for them, he didn't exist any more.

"Mom!" William hollered from upstairs. "I can't get the cap off the toothpaste."

"Coming!" She gave Adam an apologetic smile. "I'll be right back."

Lost in the darkness of the past, he stared unseeing at the fire. His mother, closeted in Marcus's bedroom with the football trophies and awards for making the honor roll, winning a debate, and being elected student council president. The polar opposite of Adam, with his after-school detentions and bad grades. Richard drunk, yelling at Adam, wishing him dead instead of Marcus.

Despite the decade-plus between then and now, old pain and regret for what had been and what was consumed Adam. He squeezed his eyes shut, but only for a moment before he got a grip. Those memories belonged in the past. He closed the door on them, but the emotions associated with them clung on.

He was on his feet again, poking at the fire, raw and ready to get the hell out of there, when William padded down the stairs in pajamas covered with colorful ninja turtles. For some reason, the sight of his clean, shiny face beneath the firefighter hat made Adam's chest hurt.

"Will you read me this story, Adam?" he asked, holding out a book.

Confused by his feelings, Adam cleared his throat. "Doesn't your mom want to do that?"

Sam shook her head. "It's okay."

The kid stared at Adam with big eyes, reminding him of a puppy. Seeing no way out, he moved to the couch and sat down. William joined him, with Sam flanking the boy's other side.

Like a family.

Adam swallowed. "The Knight and the Dragon," he read, studying the cartoon drawing on the cover. "This looks like a good book."

"It's my favorite."

As he read the story, William handed the hat to Sam and snuggled close to Adam. Warmth he didn't understand filled him, making him want things he couldn't have. Didn't deserve.

By the time he finished the book, the boy was drowsy and Sam wore a pleased smile.

Time to leave. Adam stood and ruffled William's hair. "Good night, sport."

"Will you tuck me in, Adam?"

The innocent question nearly brought him to his knees. "I can't. I have to be somewhere," he said, discomfort making him gruff.

"But—"

"He read you a story," Sam said. "That's enough."

She had no idea. "Thanks for a great meal, Sam. It's been fun, William. Don't forget to mind your mom."

"You're leaving right now?" Sam asked.

"Yeah. I'll let myself out. You get your son to bed."

As they started up the stairs, he lurched out the door.

8

"**I** wanted Adam to put me to bed," William whined while Samantha tucked the blankets around him.

Just as she'd feared, he'd quickly grown far too attached to the man. Unfortunately, so had she. Bringing William the firefighter hat, reading to him…. The man had a way with her son. And with her. What a wonderful husband and father he'd be….

Why go there when Adam didn't want a relationship and neither did she?

"He said he had to be someplace," she reminded William.

"But why did he have to?"

"Our invitation was last-minute, and he probably had plans."

Also, she'd told him twice this would be an early night. He'd certainly taken that to heart, had been so eager to leave he'd bolted out of the house before she could even say good night. Obviously, he'd had his fill of her and William.

Which came as no surprise. All the same, her feelings were hurt.

"And because he doesn't know us well enough to put you to bed," she added.

"We do so know him well enough."

"You and Adam had fun with each other tonight, but that doesn't mean he gets to come up here and tuck you in. You're my special boy, and that pleasure is reserved for me. And your grandparents, if they're around, and sometimes very close grownup friends."

"Like Mrs. Randall?"

One evening several months ago, Betty had watched William while Samantha made an emergency grocery run after a last-minute request for gluten-free scones from Guff's Lake Bed & Breakfast. On the way home, her car had broken down, and the dear woman had put him to bed. "That's right."

"Okay, Mom," William conceded, but his lower lip stuck out in disappointment. "Can we invite Adam to dinner tomorrow?"

"No."

He opened his mouth to argue, but she changed the subject. "Let's put your firefighter hat on the dresser."

"But I want to sleep with it."

"It's not that kind of hat. It'll just get in the way and keep you awake."

"Can I please keep it in bed with me?"

She couldn't deny him this small request. "Thanks for using 'please' when you asked. You may." After smoothing the covers over his little body, she set the hat beside him.

"I love you, sweetie," she murmured, planting a kiss on his upturned face. *And while other people will come and go, I will always be here for you.* "Good night and good dreams."

She switched off the overhead light, leaving the

room bathed in the glow of the honeybee nightlight her parents had given him for his fifth birthday.

In her bedroom, she traded her ankle boots for a pair of fuzzy blue socks and turned down the spread for later. The bed beckoned her, but no, not this early on a Saturday night—even if she was exhausted. Tomorrow was her one day off, and she looked forward to puttering around the house tonight without worrying about scouring the kitchen, setting out ingredients for baking, or setting the morning alarm for the wee hours. She and William could sleep in.

Downstairs again, she tidied up the living room. Adam's hat lay in the corner. Shoot, he'd forgotten it. Samantha didn't want to call or text him, not tonight.

She didn't want to think about him, period. Ignoring the hat, she carted the coffee cups and dessert plates into the kitchen. Stored the remains of William's pie in the fridge. Cleaned up the kitchen mess.

Now what?

Sipping wine and watching a movie on TV sounded good. After emptying the rest of the dinner wine into a glass, she returned to the living room. The fire had burned down, and she added another log, poking at it until the wood caught.

She plunked onto the couch and channel-surfed until she found an old movie from 1955, *On the Waterfront*, starring a young Marlon Brando. That looked interesting. Yawning, she lay down, pushing a throw pillow under her head.

According to the movie host, Brando had been thirty-one when he'd starred in the film, which made him just one year older than Adam. At that age, the actor had been one gorgeous hunk of man, but he had nothing on Adam Healey.

Forget about him. She managed that, all right, but couldn't help but grab another throw pillow and hug it close.

As riveting as the movie was, six days of averaging five hours' sleep per night had caught up to her with a vengeance. Her eyelids felt heavy. Samantha told herself to go upstairs to bed, but didn't have the energy. That was her last thought before she drifted off.

~

LESS THAN A MILE from Lucky Joe's, Adam realized he'd left his firefighter hat at Sam's. He swore.

He'd never forgotten it before. But when he'd sped away from her place, he hadn't exactly been thinking straight. He was all jumbled up inside, confused by emotions he didn't understand and didn't care to deal with. He didn't want to return to her house, but leaving his hat with her was not an option.

Grumbling, he checked for traffic, then executed a sharp U-turn. The wheels squealed and the car swerved, narrowly missing the ditch along the road.

Get a grip. Adam proceeded at a slower speed. He thought about alerting Sam that he was on his way back but decided against it. He'd run in, grab the hat, and run out—sixty seconds, max.

Twenty minutes later, he stood at her front door and punched the doorbell.

From inside, he heard the muffled sound of the chimes. He waited, but she didn't answer the door. She'd said this would be an early night, but eight-thirty? From the light blazing through a crack in the drapes, he figured she was still up.

He waited a few more beats. Then, impatient to

collect his hat and leave, he hot-leaded the bell so the chimes cascaded over themselves.

At last he heard footsteps. The door opened, and Sam squinted up at him.

"Left my fire hat behind." He didn't wait for her to ask him inside, just wiped his feet and stepped through the door.

"I know," she said. "I was going to contact you tomorrow."

In the living room, the TV was on with the sound muted. No lamps on in there, but between light from the entry, the TV screen, and the blazing fire, he could see just fine. The empty wine glass on the coffee table. Two couch pillows lying haphazardly on the rug, as if tossed down in a hurry. Sam's hair stuck up on one side, and she had a sleep-crease on the same cheek. She looked cute and sexy.

Adam's body stirred, and he knew he was in big trouble. "I woke you."

She didn't deny it. "Believe me, you did me a favor. The last time I fell asleep on the couch, I woke up in the wee hours with a sore back."

"That looks like *On the Waterfront*," he commented, nodding at the tube.

"You've seen it?"

"Several times. My pop used to be a Brando fan." Before the old man had lost himself in booze, watching classic TV movies together had been one of the few activities Adam had enjoyed sharing with him.

"It's pretty good. Or was until I drifted off." She yawned and stretched her arms out behind her, the movement thrusting her breasts forward.

She was killing him and she didn't even know it. Adam spun away and retrieved his hat from the corner.

"You left so abruptly tonight," she said. "Was it me or William?"

Neither. Both. Adam wasn't sure. "You said it would be an early evening, and he needed to get to bed. And remember, I have plans. You met Nate when you toured the station. He's in a band called Mello, and they're playing at Lucky Joe's."

"Ah. I've heard good things about Lucky Joe's, but I haven't been yet. It's not a place where I can take William."

"Do you bring him with you everywhere you go?"

"I don't exactly have a sitter. In a pinch, Betty helps out, but I don't want to take advantage of her."

He couldn't believe she didn't have someone else lined up. "You need to get out, Sam. Miranda, the secretary at the station, has a teenage daughter who could probably watch William."

"I'll keep that in mind. The truth is, even knowing I can sleep in on Sunday, I'm usually too beat to go out on a Saturday evening."

"When I'm on duty and several calls come in during the night, the next day I feel the same way."

Now that he had the hat and had spoken his piece, he should leave. He didn't.

"My son is already too attached to you," Sam said.

"Yeah, I got that feeling." Adam set the hat down again, beside her empty wine glass.

"He's already been abandoned once by his father. I don't want him to ever experience that loss and pain again."

"No one, especially a kid, should have to deal with something like that," Adam agreed.

"Then you understand why, no matter how much William wants to be around you...I can't let him."

She raised her chin and crossed her arms, once

again becoming the ferocious mama bear, bent on keeping her son safe.

But who looked out for her?

"I understand." Feeling protective himself, he gently smoothed her hair down. "There."

She groaned. "Don't tell me it was sticking up."

"A little."

"Now you've seen me at my worst. How embarrassing."

"Your worst is pretty good," he said, his renegade hand tracing her delicate ear.

She exhaled, a sweet little breath that caressed his face. Her eyelids lowered a fraction, and she leaned in.

He was short-circuiting fast, going up in flames hotter than the ones in the hearth. While he could still think, he needed to spell out a few things, make sure she understood when it came to settling down for the long-term, he was the wrong guy. "Just to be clear here, I'm not looking to get involved with you and William. Not like that."

"Then what do you want?"

Her lips parted the tiniest bit, and like always, he was lost. No longer caring that he flirted with danger, he ran his thumb over her bottom lip. "All I know is if I don't taste that mouth of yours again, I just might die."

"We can't let that happen." She cupped his face between her warm hands.

Adam's turn to close his eyes. He reveled in her touch. Desire tightened his body and an unfamiliar tenderness flooded his heart. Scared now, he blinked and stepped back, fast. "Sam, I—"

"Ssh." She pulled him down and kissed him.

9

Standing on her toes, Samantha wrapped her arms around Adam's neck and sank into the kiss. With a growl of pleasure, he rubbed his tongue against hers, cupped her hips, and pulled her tight. She could feel his erection against her stomach.

The sexiest man alive wanted her. It was a heady feeling.

His hunger fanned her own fever. Just when her knees threatened to buckle, he guided her down to the rug in front of the fire and tucked a throw pillow under her head.

"How did you know my legs were about to give out?" she whispered.

He chuckled low and deep, his eyes reflecting the firelight. "Just a lucky guess."

"Speaking of lucky... don't you have to get to Lucky Joe's?"

"Nah. At the moment, I'm right where I want to be." Leaning on his elbow, he stroked his thumb over her cheek.

"Yeah?" Smiling to herself, she turned her head and kissed his finger.

He pulled her into a searing kiss that obliterated

most of her thoughts before resting his forehead against hers. "You are so damn impossible to resist."

One dizzying kiss after another followed, until her senses filled with his taste and his desire. His hands were everywhere. Up her sides, on her breasts. Under her sweater, hot and seeking over her fevered nerves. Inside her bra, his clever fingers caging her nipples with just the right pressure.

Suddenly wet and aching between her legs, she moaned.

"It's time you got rid of that sweater and bra," Adam stated.

She sat up. So did Adam. At the same time, they removed their tops. His chest was hard and muscled, and dear God in heaven, he had washboard abs. The faded scar on his shoulder only made him more gorgeous.

"Where did this come from?" she asked, tracing the faded red line down his bicep.

"I got that a few years ago, during a nasty fire."

"It must have really hurt."

He shrugged. "All part of the job. You have beautiful breasts, Sam."

His tender expression made her feel beautiful. She leaned in and licked his nipple. Groaning, he pulled her onto his lap, so his erection pressed against her bottom.

She wrapped her thighs around his waist and clung to him as he slid backward until the wall supported him. Skin against skin. Bliss—and torture. The fine hairs on his chest teased her sensitive nipples, making her half mindless and desperate for him. She'd never wanted a man so badly.

"Touch me." She placed his hands on her needy breasts.

He was a master at pleasure. Soon his mouth replaced his hands, licking and suckling and making her restless and wild. Seeking closer contact, she shifted against his erection.

"Take it easy," he murmured, gripping her hips and forcing her to be still.

Sometime later, after deep, demanding kisses, he unfastened the button on her jeans and tugged at her zipper. The anticipation alone pushed her to the edge of a climax.

Her intense desire frightened her back to reality. She pushed his hand away. "No, Adam."

He froze, then lifted her off his lap. Suddenly shy, where mere seconds ago, she'd blatantly urged him to explore and taste her breasts, she covered them with her hands.

He reached for her sweater and bra and handed them to her. "I want you, Sam, but you're right, it's too soon."

Leaving the bra off, she pivoted from his gaze and pulled the sweater over her head. The soft wool teased her sensitized breasts still further.

When she again faced Adam, he was buttoning his shirt and watching her through slitted eyes. She couldn't help but notice that he was still aroused.

His smoldering gaze dropped to her breasts. Samantha glanced down at herself. Despite the thick wool, she could see the points of her nipples. She crossed her arms. "Don't forget your hat this time."

"I won't."

He scooped it off the coffee table, and they headed silently toward the door.

Nothing had been resolved or settled—except that they'd generated a lot of heat and longing. Samantha had no idea what the future held for them, or if there even was a future. According to Adam, probably not. Of course, she didn't want anything long-term, either.

Did she? The common-sense part of her brain warned her that no, getting involved could hurt William. Where had it been an hour ago?

Stunned by the depth of her passion, she opened the door, relishing the crisp, cold air that rushed over her hot skin. "Good night, Adam."

"I'll call you soon."

He brushed his lips over hers, a quick and sweet good night, before he disappeared into the darkness.

∾

MONDAY MORNING, Adam drove toward Guff's Lake Medical Clinic for his nine-thirty doctor's appointment. His ankle had just about healed, and his wrist got better by the day. With any luck, Dr. Fowler would clear him to get back on regular duty.

Traffic was light, and his mind wandered. To Sam and Saturday night.

Fooling around with her had given him a taste of her passion, which he wanted to thoroughly explore. Her responsiveness and eagerness turned him on. Even now, recalling the little sounds of pleasure she made when he'd touched and tasted her breasts made him hard.

He shifted in his seat. "Settle down, hear?" he ordered his unwanted erection.

Despite an almost constant hard-on, courtesy of Sam, he was in great spirits. So good that not even the old man had dampened his mood this morning.

Not about to wonder at what—or who—to thank for his positive frame of mind, he turned into the clinic parking lot, pulled into a vacant slot, and killed the engine.

He rode the elevator to Dr. Fowler's office on the second floor. As usual, patients packed the waiting area. Adam checked in and found a seat. Minutes later, Martha, one of the doctor's assistants, called his name. He followed her to an exam room.

She'd worked here forever, at least since the good doctor had given Adam a physical and the all-clear required by the Guff's Lake Fire Department when he'd first applied for the job. He couldn't tell her age, but she looked a couple years older than Dr. Fowler.

"How you doing, Adam?" she asked as she took his weight and blood pressure.

"Not bad. I'll be even better if the doc clears me for regular duty."

"I hope he does. Be good, y'hear?"

He answered her standard refrain with his usual reply. "You know I can't promise that."

As he'd anticipated, she shook her head and grinned. "You're hopeless. Have a seat on the exam table. Dr. Fowler will be in shortly."

Not long after she exited the room, the silver-haired doctor entered with Adam's chart. He gave a brisk nod then washed his hands. "Good to see you, Adam. Let's take a look at your wrist."

Having ditched his bandage in the car in order to look all healed up, Adam held out his arm.

"Any pain?" Dr. Fowler asked, prodding the area of the sprain.

Yeah, but for the sake of returning to work, Adam stifled a wince and shook his head. "Feels okay."

The doctor jotted something on Adam's chart and then checked his ankle. "That ankle looks good as new."

"It doesn't bother me at all anymore. Can I go back to regular duty?"

"If you had a less rigorous job, I'd say yes, but you still have quite a bit of bruising and swelling on your wrist. I'm not going to clear you just yet."

Well, hell. Should've skipped cleaning the old man's gutters. When he found out about this, he'd no doubt make some snarky comment about Adam being a wimp or other more-derogatory names—unless he'd forgotten about this morning's appointment. Not likely, as Adam had reminded him.

"How much longer do I have to wait, Doc?"

"Come back in a week. Meanwhile, baby that wrist."

Adam left the clinic in a far worse mood than when he'd entered. The captain had given him half the day off for his appointment, and he still had several hours before he needed to be at the station. If he was smart, he'd go home and hit the books.

Instead, he headed for Sam's.

10

A s soon as Samantha stepped through the door after dropping William at kindergarten Monday morning, she made a beeline for her coffee pot. She'd already had her quota—one cup after stumbling into the kitchen to bake in the early morning, and a second while she and William made their deliveries. Today, she needed an extra caffeine boost. She filled a mug and set it the microwave to heat.

While she waited, she thought about pulling the heavy café curtains open to let in the cheery light. But she didn't have the energy.

If only she'd turned in early last night. Instead, scouring the kitchen and assembling the needed ingredients for this morning's baking had taken longer than usual, thanks to the tantalizing thoughts of Adam Healey that had distracted her.

His big hands, strong and callused, yet gentle and knowing. His mouth, his hard, muscled body... Her nipples sharpened, and a longing ache bloomed between her legs.

"Stop it," she ordered herself in a stern voice.

What was the point of fantasizing when she didn't

even know if she'd ever see him again? So she'd reasoned with herself countless times in the last twenty-
four hours. For all the good that did.

The microwave beeped. With a weary sigh, she sat
down with her coffee and the recipe box she'd started
in eighth-grade home ec, when she'd first discovered
the joys of cooking. In no time, she found the cookie
recipe she wanted.

As she set out the butter to soften, the doorbell
rang. Expecting an order of supplies from one of her
mail-order wholesalers, she wiped her hands on her
jeans and hurried to the door.

Instead of finding the usual balding deliveryman
on the porch, she found Adam. Dressed in faded jeans
and his bomber jacket over a black T-shirt, he looked
fit and handsome.

"Hey," he said, leaning against the doorjamb.

Talk about your heart-palpitating pose. His avid
gaze swept over her jeans and sweatshirt, warming her
wherever it lit. There went her nipples, tightening
with longing. Again.

Absently, she fluffed her hair. "Aren't you supposed to be at the doctor's?"

"I just left there. I was going to call, but I decided
to stop by instead. Mind if I come in?"

The last time he'd waltzed inside, Samantha had
ended up enjoying the most arousing kisses and caresses of her life. Kisses and caresses that messed with
her mind, keeping her from much-needed rest and
making her want to throw caution to the winds, ignore
common sense, and let physical desire lead the way.

So yes, she minded. Or so she attempted to convince herself. With her rational mind doing battle
with her *Let's take up where we left off* body, that proved
challenging.

While she silently duked it out with herself, Adam exhaled heavily. It wasn't a happy sound. He looked so disappointed, Samantha couldn't send him away. She stepped back and gestured him inside.

"I'm guessing the appointment didn't go as you'd hoped," she commented when he shut the door behind him.

Or maybe he regretted what had happened Saturday night and wanted to apologize and forget all about those kisses and caresses. Which would be for the best. Only Samantha didn't want to stop. Score one for body over rational mind.

Adam shrugged out of his jacket and hung it on the doorknob of the coat closet. "The doctor wouldn't clear me. He scheduled me for another exam next week."

Not a word about the other night. Relieved, she let out a breath of her own. "Eventually, he'll let you go back."

"He'd better."

"You still have to be at work for light duty, right?"

"Not until noon." Adam sniffed the air. "I smell coffee and treats."

Something in his expression reminded her of an eager little boy, and she couldn't help laughing. "Down, big guy," she teased. "I baked at oh-dark thirty this morning, and delivered every last scone, muffin, and cinnamon roll to my customers. There's nothing left over to feed you. As for the coffee, I made it hours ago."

She hated how his face fell. "Although I do happen to have a few treats stashed in the freezer, things that taste good, but aren't pretty enough to sell. I can offer you a raspberry muffin or an orange scone and a cup of reheated coffee."

"How about a scone and a muffin with that coffee?"

"You got it."

While she warmed his snack in the microwave, Adam plunked into a chair at the kitchen table. "Did I mention that my pop goes crazy for your muffins?"

"You did."

"Lately, they're about the only thing he enjoys," he grumbled.

"Well, he is sick."

"True, but happiness has never been his strong suit." Adam nodded at the recipe box and changed the subject. "What's that?"

"Recipes for personal use." She traded the plate of warmed treats for the mug of cold coffee and reset the microwave.

When Adam had his food and drink, she sat down across from him.

"This is exactly what I needed," he said around a large mouthful. "My mom had one of these recipe boxes, but I don't remember that she ever used it. Her idea of cooking has always been takeout, pizza, or frozen dinners."

That sounded terrible, but the woman had lost a son and suffered through what sounded like an unhappy marriage. Not everyone found cooking and baking to be healing and comforting. Samantha did, and when Jeff had walked out, she'd filled the house with delicious meals and desserts.

Adam scanned the card she'd pulled out, and licked his lips. "Double chocolate cookies—sounds great."

The man had a serious sweet tooth.

"They're William's favorites. I'm bribing him with them. If he takes a nap today, I'll make them and he gets to help. That means licking the spoon and the bowl."

"Hell, for a chance to lick the bowl, I'd take a nap. He's a lucky kid."

"As I remind him daily." She smiled. "Did you enjoy Nate's band the other night?"

"I didn't go. After I left you, I didn't feel like being around other people."

His eyes went bright and hot. Samantha's most sensitive parts started to hum, and she forgot all about how exhausted she was.

"I keep remembering what we did," she admitted.

"Same here. Are you sorry?"

"No. Are you?"

His eyes locked on hers and he shook his head, and every cell in her body strained toward him.

"But I would like to know where this is going." Although at the moment, she couldn't think beyond her immediate physical desire.

"I can't get you out of my head, Sam. How good we already are together."

He reached across the table and traced her bottom lip with his treacherous thumb, almost obliterating what was left of her common sense.

"I want to be inside you."

Yes! her body shouted. But she wasn't ready for that just yet. "It's too soon."

"Copy that." He dropped his hand. "We could still fool around."

She could no more turn that tempting offer down than stop breathing. The instant she nodded, Adam stood, moved around the table, clasped her hands, and pulled her to her feet. She melted into his arms.

～

SAM WAS WARM AND SOFT, and she smelled amazing. Holding nothing back, Adam kissed her. She responded with an eagerness that blew him away. A certain part of him jumped to attention and demanded release. He wanted to head straight upstairs, bury himself in her sweetness, and put an end to this physical torment.

But she'd just told him she wasn't ready. Still kissing her, he backed her toward a cluttered trestle table in the hallway. Impatient to put the table to his own use, he set her purse on the floor and cleared what was left with a sweep of his hand.

Sam jerked back. "What are you doing?"

"That's for me to know and you to find out." With a teasing smile, he lifted her up and set her down.

"I'm all intrigued." She pulled him down for a sizzling kiss.

He stepped between her thighs, gratified when she tilted forward, bringing them as close as a fully-clothed man and woman could get. It wasn't close enough. Adam ground into her. Her fevered moan almost did him in. About to embarrass himself, he stepped back.

"I can't get enough of you. Your mouth. Your breasts." He tugged her sweatshirt up and pulled it over her head.

She unhooked the bra herself. As he pulled one tight nipple into his mouth, her head fell back against the wall. Giving her pleasure turned him on, and he took his time on each breast. Restless, she shifted in his arms. Adam undid the button on her jeans. The subtle tension in her body gave him pause. She still might not be ready for what he had in mind.

He hesitated. "You okay with this?"

"Yes," she whispered.

Working the zipper down, he dipped inside the elastic band of her panties. When he reached the place where they both wanted him to be, she was already wet for him. She raised one hip and then the other, tacitly encouraging him to get rid of the jeans and panties.

For a long moment, he looked her over, this gorgeous woman naked and aroused.

Eager to get back to the good stuff, he knelt between her legs, pulled her toward him and parted her folds to fully reveal her sex. "You are so beautiful," he said, hearing the hoarseness in his own voice.

"Down there? You've got to be kidding me."

"Trust me, you are."

He leaned down and flicked his tongue over her most sensitive part. She made one of those catchy, breathy sounds that drove him mad.

"You like that," he said, pausing to look up at her.

"A lot."

He slid two fingers into her slickness. "And this?"

"Dear God, yes."

He went back to business. Moments later, she grabbed onto his ears, moaned, and let go.

On the edge himself, Adam almost came with her. Somehow, he held back. He would save that for when he was deep inside her.

As unsatisfied as he was, he couldn't help but grin when he handed her the sweatshirt and pushed to his feet.

For a moment, she disappeared inside it. Then she slid off the table. The shirt hung about halfway down her bare thigh. Sexy.

"I enjoyed that almost as much as you did," he said. Every shuddering moment.

She blushed, deepening her already-flushed skin.

"I haven't been with a man in a while." She stepped into her panties and then pulled on her jeans.

"How long?"

"Since a few months before Jeff walked out."

"That's a long time."

"True, but until now, I haven't been interested."

Adam was pleased that she'd chosen him to end her self-imposed celibacy.

She eyed the erection straining his fly. "That looks uncomfortable."

It was. "I'll survive."

He gathered her purse and the scattered books and notebooks from the floor, and returned all of it to the table. "It's about time for you to pick up William."

Sam glanced at her watch. "I didn't realize what time it was. I'd better scoot or I'll be late."

They left the house together. In the cold, gray morning, the breath flew from their lips like double smoke plumes, before trailing away.

They were almost at Adam's car. He moved in to kiss her good-bye, but she gave her head a vigorous shake and pushed him away.

"Not out here, when Betty Randall could drive or walk by at any time. As much as I love the woman, she tends to have a big mouth, and I don't want to do anything to fuel gossip that could hurt William."

No sooner had she spoken than a cream-color sedan turned onto the street.

Samantha groaned. "Speak of the devil."

Her gray-haired neighbor slowed, waved, and pulled to a stop. "More plumbing problems?"

"Plumbing?" Adam repeated.

"She saw you at the door the day you replaced the washer in the faucet," Sam said under her breath. She offered the woman in the idling car a bright smile. "Hi, Betty. This is Adam Healey."

Betty checked him out. "I knew I recognized you when I saw you before. You're not a plumber, you're Mr. January."

"Yeah, and I know my way around a leaky faucet. Nice to meet you."

"Likewise." She batted her lashes.

"Adam's on his way out, and so am I," Sam said.

"I have to go, too. I'm sure I'll see you again, Adam. Bye, Samantha." With a knowing look, Betty drove away.

Shaking her head, Sam accompanied him to the 4Runner. "Did you see how she flirted with you?"

"Oh, I noticed. She has to be twenty years older than my mother. Women just can't resist me," he joked.

Sam laughed. "You are so full of yourself!"

Liking that happy sound, he shrugged and grinned. More than anything, he wanted to brush the bangs from her eyes and kiss her until, once again, they were both half out of their minds. But he had to get to work, and she needed to pick up her son.

"I hope Betty didn't get the wrong idea," Sam said. "When William takes his nap this afternoon, I'm going to call her and straighten things out."

"A cinnamon roll and a muffin might help." Adam opened his car door. "I don't have clock in until ten tomorrow. Why don't I stop by before work."

"I'll be here."

Before he even pulled away from the curb, he was anticipating his next visit.

11

When Jana picked Samantha up for knitting Thursday morning, she seemed a little down.

"I know that sad face," Samantha said. "Don't tell me that you and Jon—"

"Broke up. Yep."

Her friend turned the car around. They'd only been dating a month, and she'd never said anything about loving him, but it was clear she was hurt all the same. Samantha gave her a sympathetic look. "Poor you."

"It's my fault for jumping into bed with him on the third date. If I'd only waited, I could have saved myself a lot of grief." Jana sighed and turned onto Kirkdale Road. "Next time, I swear I'll wait at least six weeks before I let a guy get intimate. If I don't, feel free to slap me, hard."

"I'll stick with a reminder instead. Why don't you come over for ice cream and cookies Saturday night? We'll watch TV and gorge ourselves."

"That's sweet, but my sister offered to treat me to dinner and a movie. Listen, I don't want to talk about my messed-up love life anymore. I'd rather talk about you." Jana gave a sly smile. "I hear that things are heating up between you and Adam."

Understatement of the world.

For the past three mornings, Adam had stopped by after Samantha dropped off William and before he went to work. They sat across the kitchen table, sipping coffee, eating treats, and talking about everything. Adam's dad, who sounded like a very difficult man. Samantha's parents, who, even during a call last week, had pressured her to contact Jeff and make up with him. William, Adam's progress with his class and studies, her baking business, and whatever else came up.

But the best part of their time together happened after the snack, when they continued with what they'd started and couldn't seem to stop. Samantha still wasn't ready for sex, but with every passing day, she and Adam skated closer to making love. They both knew it was only a matter of time before she invited him into her bed.

Samantha slanted her friend a look. "How did you know about Adam and me?"

"Let's just say that his 4Runner has been spotted in your driveway more than once."

"Betty Randall." Samantha groaned. "I knew I should have knocked on her door and explained."

Which she couldn't do when William refused to nap. For a full week now, despite cookies and other attempted bribes, he wouldn't even lie down. Samantha guessed he'd outgrown his need for an afternoon rest. He was getting bigger every day.

She should have run over to Betty's yesterday or the day before, during kindergarten. Instead, she'd been with Adam.

"Talking to her would only backfire," Jana pointed

out. "It's a known fact she likes to be the one in the know."

"But we're friends," Samantha said.

"Even so, no matter what you tell her, you'll only make things worse."

"You're probably right." Samantha grew pensive. "I wonder who she told."

"All I know is, she had a hair appointment at Tommie's Hair and Nails yesterday, with Carol Sue."

The popular hairstylist happened to be every bit as nosey as Betty. "She may as well have rented a megaphone and shouted out the news to the whole town." Samantha groaned again. "I moved to Guff's Lake because I assumed this town was too big for the busybody gossip that thrives in Enterprise."

They were about two miles from Deb's now, and Jana braked to a stop for a red light. "Twenty thousand-odd people isn't exactly a big city."

"Compared to the five thousand in Enterprise it is."

"Doesn't matter. Around here, gossip is the spice of life. Now, back to Adam. Exactly when did you decide to make time for a man in your life? Because I'm supposed to be your best friend, and I sure didn't hear about it."

Samantha had wanted to keep the fact they were seeing each other to herself. "You and I are both so busy," she said. "I haven't had time to call you. Besides, this isn't something Adam and I planned. We just sort of fell into it."

"From the sparks you two generated at Rosemary's the day you met, I should have guessed."

"Not even I could have guessed. I swear, it's not that big a deal." Samantha wasn't about to share what she and Adam did together. "Neither of us wants any-thing long-term."

"Who cares if you are or ever will be serious? The point is, right now, Adam Healey is interested in you. Trust me, there are plenty of women in town who'd love to snag his attention, even for a little while. Including yours truly. If I was in your shoes, I'd broadcast the news myself."

"You don't have a son who could get hurt."

Jana looked confused.

"William has seen Adam exactly three times. That day we met him at Rosemary's, again when we toured the station, and then when Adam came to dinner Saturday night. He—"

"Hold on, there. You invited Adam over for dinner?"

"Actually, William did."

"Really." Jana almost sang the word. She sounded way too happy.

Samantha hastened to explain. "It was just a simple meal, a thank-you for showing William and me around the station. I didn't go to any trouble, except to set an extra place at the table." If you didn't count that they'd eaten in the dining room or that Samantha had worn the jeans and sweater she knew flattered her. "William hasn't stopped talking about him since."

He mentioned Adam at least twice a day. Samantha had begun to think Betty was right—her son needed a father figure. "I don't want him growing too attached, so when Adam left Saturday night, I told William we wouldn't be seeing him anymore."

"Only you are seeing him."

"But William doesn't know." Samantha gnawed the pad of her thumb. "If he found out Adam has been coming over while he's in kindergarten instead of when he's home... I don't know what he'd think. He's been rejected once, and I can't let him suffer through that ever again. Besides, Adam and I don't have a future together."

"William would get hurt." Jana gave a sympathetic nod. "I get that."

"And now Betty has gone and told people about Adam and me." She knocked her forehead against the passenger window. "Why didn't I tell him to go away?" Because she hadn't been able to stop herself. She wanted him that much. "What if William hears something?"

"From whom?" Jana pulled into the parking lot and parked in a slot in front of Deb's Knitting Store. "He's a little kid. He won't."

On the heels of her words, the clouds parted and sunlight burst into the car. Samantha took that as a good omen. Maybe Jana was right.

~

AROUND THE TABLE at the back of Deb's Knitting Store, hands flew, needles click-clacked and stitches accumulated as Samantha and the four other women in class chatted and worked on their various projects. Except for Deb, the married fifty-something owner of the store, they were all about the same age and all single.

Becca Chambers, owner of Second Hand Rose, glanced at Samantha. "So, you and Adam Healey are a thing now."

Every woman paused mid-purl and wide-eyed her.

Samantha concentrated on pulling out a row of the sweater that would not end, where she'd somehow dropped a stitch. "We aren't exactly 'a thing,' but we have been seeing each other."

"Adam Healey. Now there's a man." Hallie Sawyer, a freelance writer and a decent knitter, exhaled dreamily over her half-finished pink angora sweater.

Collective sighs filled the air, including Deb's.

"Samantha doesn't want anyone to know about the thing with Adam," Jana said. She didn't seem at all bothered by Samantha's "Shut it" glare.

Everyone looked confused. "Explain about William," Jana said.

Advice from her friends could help. Samantha told them about Jeff. She segued to her son's quick attachment to Adam and finished with exactly what she'd told Jana.

Deb nodded thoughtfully and bent over the cutest baby blanket. "You never know, you just might be the one woman Adam can't get enough of. And he might be the perfect man for you."

"Wouldn't that be something?" Becca murmured, shaking her head.

So much for advice. Samantha wished they'd all stop acting as if she and Adam were an actual couple.

"Don't talk about Adam and me as if we're together. We aren't," she chided. "And please, if you hear anything to the contrary, set people straight."

The women promised they would. The talk turned to knitting, and after a moment, Samantha relaxed.

Still, she couldn't quite shake the feeling that no matter what they said, people would continue to talk.

12

F riday morning, Adam whistled as he took the
porch steps two at a time to Sam's front door.
He'd missed not seeing her the day before,
plus he wanted to tell her about his lawyer buddy.

Seconds after he rang the doorbell, she answered.

"Hey," he said, wiping his feet.

She barely opened the door enough to stick her
head out. "I don't think you should come in."

The frown tugging at the corners of her mouth
puzzled Adam. He squinted at her. "Are you sick?"

"It's worse than that." She stepped outside and ran
her hand through her hair. After a cautious glance up
and down the street, she lowered her voice. "Everyone
in town knows you've been coming over while William
is at kindergarten."

He scoffed. "I doubt that."

"The women in my kitting class found out, and
guess how? Betty had a hair appointment with Carol
Sue."

Familiar with the hairdresser and her motor
mouth, Adam grimaced.

"It's only a matter of time before William finds
out," Sam said.

He swore. "Your neighbor should keep her nose out of our business. Now, can we go inside?"

"No, and I don't want you to come over anymore."

"At all?"

"That's right. Why give Betty or anyone else more to gossip about?"

Feeling gobsmacked, Adam shook his head. He enjoyed being with Sam, talking to her and eating her baked goods. Best of all, he liked the sweet sounds she made when he touched her. When he took her sky-high and she let go. They hadn't had sex yet, but they were getting closer.

He definitely did not want to stop coming around.

He stamped his feet, his boots making a loud thud against the porch's wood planks. "We need to talk, and it's too cold to stand out here. If you won't let me in, let's go someplace and get coffee."

"So that more people see us together? No."

Okay, then. "You want to sit in my car?"

Sam shook her head and gave a resigned sigh. "You may as well come in."

After shooting a wary look around for signs of nosey Betty, he entered the house. As always, he shrugged out of his jacket and as always, hung it on the doorknob of the coat closet. He didn't smell fresh coffee or warming treats. To his disappointment, instead of heading for the kitchen, Sam went straight to the living room.

Adam plunked himself onto the couch, where he and Sam had fooled around on his last visit. She chose an armchair.

"C'mon, Sam, I promise not to bite." He patted the cushion beside him.

"All right, but no kissing or touching." She tucked

herself into the corner, as far away from him as possible.

He muttered a few choice words. "Even if Betty strolls past the house, she can't see in here...unless she sneaks into the backyard and looks through the window."

He thought Sam might crack a smile. She didn't.

"She's too busy to bother today," she said. "She's out shopping for presents for her grandchildren for an upcoming trip. At least that's what she said when I called her last night."

"Did you tell her to butt out of our business?"

"I explained about William. She hadn't considered him, and she apologized for saying anything. But it's too late now."

"If she's going out of town..."

"She doesn't leave for a couple more weeks."

"We can meet at my place," he suggested. "No one in my neighborhood cares who I see or what I do."

"I don't think so."

Suddenly, he understood. This wasn't about William or the nosey neighbor. Sam had lost interest in him. Coming out of the blue this way, it packed a real wallop.

Not about to show his bruised feelings, he used a trick he'd perfected after Marcus had died—he schooled his expression into bland indifference. "If you don't want to see me anymore, just come out and say it."

"Oh, I'm still interested." Her expressive eyes, always easy to read, underlined the words.

This was great news. The tension that had put knots in his belly eased. He started to move closer, but she held up her hands, palms up.

"I have to protect my son."

"What's to protect? He doesn't know about us."

"Not yet, but with people talking, it's only a matter of time. I don't want him thinking you're going to be part of his life."

There was that. Adam didn't want to cause the boy pain or let him down. After screwing up so bad with Richard, he didn't need this on his conscience, too. But he still wanted to see Sam.

He scratched the back of his neck. "What if we explain that we're good friends and make sure William understands?"

"Is that what we are, Adam? Friends?"

"Well, yeah." Maybe a little more than that. "Plus, we have great chemistry."

The look she gave him... Longing and heat. Oh, yeah, major chemistry.

In that moment, he'd never wanted a woman as much as he wanted Sam. Ignoring her orders to keep his hands to himself, he slid over and kissed her gently. "I don't want to stop seeing you, Sam."

"Oh, Adam, me, either. If it weren't for William..." She gave him a sad smile. "Even if we swear we're only friends, he's bound to get his hopes up. In the end, he'll get hurt. For his sake, we have to stop."

For several glum minutes, neither of them said a word.

This seemed a good time to change the subject. "I ran into a buddy of mine yesterday, a lawyer named Dwight Cornell. He helped me with my divorce all those years ago, and since then, he's worked with some of the guys at the station when their marriages fell apart. I mentioned that you need legal advice about your ex. He said to call." He fished Cornell's business card from his hip pocket and handed it over.

"Thanks." Sam set it on the coffee table. "As soon as I save up the money, I'll contact him."

"You don't need any money up front, not with Dwight. As a friend of mine, you can figure out the payment schedule that works best for you."

"I'm still paying off debt from the divorce. I don't need to add more. You'd better go."

Adam gave a reluctant nod.

They both stood and headed for the door. Seconds later, standing in the entry with his jacket on, he touched her cheek. "Take care, Sam."

~

AFTER A LOUSY WEEKEND—ADAM missed Sam, and he'd lost at the Friday night poker game—he finally caught a break Monday morning. Dr. Fowler green-lighted him to return to his regular shift.

Adam was elated. Captain Comings had given him the okay to come in at noon, more than an hour from now. He thought about stopping by Sam's and sharing the good news, but they'd agreed he should steer clear.

He stopped at his pop's with the expected muffin to let him know he wouldn't be back until Wednesday, waiting until the muffin disappeared. "I've been cleared for regular duty, so you won't see me tomorrow. I'll stop by with your muffin Wednesday morning."

"So, it's back to the salt mines for you."

His father's attention never wavered from the Swiffer commercial on the tube, making it clear that he preferred the lame ad to Adam's company.

Never mind. Once he made lieutenant, Richard

would look at him differently—would look at him, period.

"See you, Pop," Adam muttered.

On the drive to the station, he donned his Bluetooth and dialed Sam. She didn't want to see him, but they hadn't discussed phone calls.

"Adam." She sounded surprised.

Her voice worked its magic on him, winding its sweetness through his gut and filling him with familiar hunger. God above, he wanted to be with her. "Hey."

"Hi."

Then, silence.

He waited for her to say she missed him, that she'd changed her mind and wanted him to hurry over. She didn't.

He cleared his throat. "Dr. Fowler okayed me to go back to work. I'll be clocking in at noon."

"Hooray! You start today?"

"Yep." His ferocious need and frustration made him terse.

"But your shift begins at eight in the morning."

"That's right. I'll make up the rest of the hours later. Tell William for me. He'll want to know."

"I will. Thanks for calling, Adam."

She acted as if he were an acquaintance, not the man who'd seen her naked and lost in the throes of passion.

In a crappy mood, Adam disconnected. As he drove toward the station, he forced his mind to the day ahead. It'd be good to be a part of the crew again. Between work, hanging with the guys, and studying after dinner, he'd have no time to fantasize about Sam.

13

On a slow Monday afternoon a week after Adam returned to his regular shift, Rafe clapped him on the shoulder. "Up for a workout?"

They all liked to keep fit and, time permitting, they worked out in the station's gym.

"Hell, yeah."

By the time Adam changed into shorts and a T-shirt, Rafe, Daniel, Rob, Ethan, and Owen were already hard at it. Captain Comings, Hank, Max, Tony, Gus, Nate, and Liam had just finished up.

Sweating and grunting and straining, Adam put himself through all the paces and then some. After some two months off, he needed it. Plus, with the required physical test required for the promotion just around the corner, he had to kick his ass back into shape, fast.

When he finished, he felt great, ready for whatever came his way. And plenty did.

Two fires, one in the dead of night. Tuesday morning, seriously sleep-deprived but coping, he drove to Orchard High, his alma mater, to conduct a safety training assembly.

At the end, a girl and two boys approached him about becoming firefighters.

"It's a competitive field," he said, "but we're always looking for qualified candidates."

"How do we get qualified?" the taller, skinner of the two boys asked.

"Earn good grades. Enroll in college and take fire safety classes. Work toward your paramedics degree, and volunteer at the county station. Then come see us."

The girl jotted down his every word. Short and curvy, with bangs that hung in her eyes, she reminded him a little of Sam.

So it figured that on the drive back to the station, he thought about Sam. Her pretty smile and the way her laugh coaxed out his own. Her expressive eyes and their easy back-and-forth. How she bit her lip or gnawed the pad of her thumb when something bothered her. Her dedication to her work and her amazing baking skills. Her devotion to William. And her passion.

He caught himself in a sappy grin. With a shock, he realized he liked her a whole lot more than he'd ever intended.

"Damn," he muttered. He didn't want to care this much. Sam didn't want that, either.

Irritated, he shoved her from his mind. For all the good that did.

Dinner was always a community affair, with each man taking a turn at cooking dinner for the others. Tony was tonight's chef. He served up fried chicken with all the fixings—mountains of food. And a good thing, with the captain and twelve hungry firefighters to feed. Anyone who made the mistake of stiffing on food got razzed mercilessly and never did it again.

Sitting around the big, rectangular table, they helped themselves and dug in.

"Good chicken," Gus commented when he came up for air and dished up seconds. Built like a linebacker, he really packed it away.

Adam's crewmates ate and joked and laughed, as they usually did. Adam joined in, but without his usual enthusiasm. He figured no one noticed. Then Liam eyed him with his infamous scowl.

"You're in a crappy mood. You said you couldn't wait to come back. It's only been a week, and you're glaring at the world."

The rest of the men, even Captain Comings, fixed him with hard stares. He snorted. "You need to see an eye doctor and get yourself some glasses."

Rafe smirked. "Two words. Samantha Everett."

Adam narrowed his eyes, and the joker hooted. "I knew it."

"Shut up and pass the mashed potatoes."

"So, it's like that." Ethan gave a sage nod.

Adam piled potatoes onto his plate. "The problem is William. His dad is out of the picture, and he's growing a little too attached to me."

Rafe shook his head. "This is exactly why I steer clear of single moms."

"Amen," several of the other men seconded.

The room grew quiet, everyone too busy eating to comment. Figuring he'd dodged a bullet, Adam relaxed.

"I remember William from when you showed him and Sam around the station," Liam said, and Adam tensed up again. "Cute kid. Even then, he looked at you with stars in his eyes. Like you were his hero."

Between the tour and the instant attraction between him and Sam, Adam hadn't noticed. Even if he had, nothing would have changed. He still would have pursued Sam. "I'm no hero, and I sure as hell can't be William's."

Nate looked thoughtful. "Kids are great, until they turn into teenagers. Then they get pretty weird and dramatic...at least my girls do." Divorced, with twin fifteen-year-old daughters, he knew firsthand.

"Yeah, but they're yours," Rob said. "When they're some other guy's..."

A long, noisy exchange followed, guys speaking their minds and sometimes disagreeing. Finally, they quieted down.

Max eyed Adam. "What are you gonna do about Sam?"

"How the hell should I know?" Adam drained his water glass to avoid having to say more.

Rafe snorted. "Does she know you have feelings for her?"

Uncomfortable discussing his feelings, Adam rolled his eyes. "I'm trying to finish my dinner."

"Suit yourself, man. But if it was me, I'd go over there and try to work something out."

SAMANTHA HAD JUST FINISHED TUCKING her sleepy son in after a bedtime story Tuesday evening, when he regarded her with the big, somber-eyed expression that always melted her heart.

"Mom?"

"Yes, sweetie?"

"Do you think Adam misses me?"

It had been more than a week since Adam had called to say he'd been cleared for work, and longer than that since William had last seen him. But her son couldn't seem to forget the firefighter. "I'm sure he does."

"Then why doesn't he come and see me?"

William looked crestfallen. Aching for him and wishing she'd done a better job protecting him, she forced a smile and smoothed his furrowed brow. "You remember why...because he's super busy."

Samantha missed Adam, too, more than she would ever let on to her son. With the exception of that one call, she hadn't heard from him. Not even a text or an email.

She ought to be relieved he'd taken their decision to not see each other seriously. But couldn't the man at least try to change her mind?

Now that he was back on his regular shift, he'd probably forgotten all about her. When she really liked him—and more.

Truth be told, she was half in love with the man.

That should have terrified her. Did. But she couldn't control her heart any more than the chilly February weather.

"Could we go see him at the station tomorrow?" William asked.

Adam didn't work Wednesdays. Even if he did, she didn't want him thinking she was chasing after him. Besides, seeing him again would only set William up for more disappointment.

"Mrs. Randall asked us to visit Gordy and Cocoa while she's visiting her family in Portland. I thought we'd go over tomorrow," she said, hoping to distract her son with the horses.

"Okay, but when can we visit Adam?"

He just wouldn't give up. Samantha blew out a breath. "Let's talk about this later. It's late and we have to be up early." She kissed his forehead. "Good night and good dreams."

Feeling lonely and very sorry for herself, she plodded down the stairs to prep for tomorrow's baking. In the kitchen, she turned the radio to her favorite oldies station, donned a bib apron and hair net, and then washed her hands.

While she measured and mixed dry ingredients together, she continued to wonder about Adam. Was he fighting a fire? Treating someone with a medical emergency, studying, or playing cards with his friends? Regardless, he probably wasn't thinking about her.

Her heart ached. But then, he'd never promised her anything. Still, she'd assumed he cared, simply by the warmth in his eyes and his tenderness toward her. Behavior rooted in more than physical need. Otherwise, he would have walked away as soon as she refused to make love. Wouldn't he?

When the radio began its on-the-hour news update, Samantha realized she'd wasted precious time lost in an endless loop of what-ifs. Painful experience had taught her wishful thinking never solved anything.

"Enough of that," she stated out loud. Straightening her shoulders, she set to work.

14

N ot long after dinner, Adam decided to call it a night. After a busy day, he expected to fall into dreamland the second his head hit the pillow. Instead, he tossed and turned and longed for Sam.

He wasn't supposed to miss her like this.

She didn't want him to, either—or so she'd claimed. Yet she'd kissed him, responded to him, looked at him with a hell of a lot of something that went way beyond the physical.

When a woman started to fall for him, he usually cut and run. But this time... He wasn't used to such deep feelings.

Feelings. Scary stuff, risky at best.

All the same, he cared.

What was he supposed to do with that?

Rafe's words echoed in his mind. *If it was me, I'd go over there, tell the woman how I felt, and see if we could work something out.*

Not a bad idea, if this was about just Sam and him. If she didn't have William.

Of all the single women in the world, he had to get interested in one with a kid.

Adam punched the pillow hard, surprised when the casing didn't break apart. Resting his head on his arms, he stared into the darkness. Stupid, weak bastard, damn fool. None of the names with which he taunted himself, labels the old man had once scarred into his mind on a daily basis, changed the fact he wanted Sam.

He hooted out loud, the sound more like an anguished howl. Then he dismissed Rafe's advice. No, thanks. He preferred to steer clear.

With that, he rolled over and finally slept.

OFTEN IN THE QUIET, early morning hours, Samantha caught up on email and text messages while she waited for whatever was in the oven to bake.

On this dark Wednesday morning, Jana had texted a photo of the shoulder bag she wanted to knit, a pattern that looked a lot easier than the sweater that would not end. Getting the sleeves right tried Samantha's patience to the max, but darn it, she would knit them into submission. A supplier had emailed a delivery date for an order, and a friend in Enterprise had forwarded a joke. Just the usual stuff.

Until the last email of the bunch. It was from Jeff, and stopped her cold.

It's been awhile. We need to talk, and I want to see William. I'll be in Guff's Lake next week and will contact you when I arrive.

Samantha gaped at the message. Why now when she'd finally moved on and started a new life? As far as she knew, since the divorce, Jeff hadn't visited Enterprise or contacted any of the people they'd once counted as friends. Then how had he learned she'd moved to Guff's Lake?

More important, why did he want to talk to her?

Panic mounting, she attempted to reason with herself. Jeff was William's father, and as much as she detested him, it might be good for William to see him.

To open old wounds and cause him pain all over again? *Oh, hell no.*

On the heels of that, something awful popped into her mind. That Jeff planned to take her son away.

Fear shuddered through her. Suddenly chilled to the bone and unable to sit still, she jumped up and paced to the kitchen window. Hugging herself, she stared out, at the darkness. *Please, oh please, don't let him come after William.*

The buzzing timer jerked her back to the present. The act of pulling two pans of muffins from the oven and then sliding two more in calmed her enough to reason.

Two clear thoughts filled her mind. One, Jeff would never take her son. She raised her trembling chin. *Just let him try.* And two, she was pretty sure who had told him where to find her. Her mother.

Anger overshadowed the fear. Samantha compressed her lips and narrowed her eyes. She wanted to call her mom right away and ream her out, but at this hour, her parents were sure to be sleeping. They didn't get up until seven, and they left for Everett's General Store around eight. She would contact them after she dropped William at kindergarten.

Mind whirling and heart pounding, she finished baking, and then packed and loaded the orders into the car. She got William up and dressed, survived the morning deliveries, and smilingly dropped him at kindergarten.

At home again, she speed-dialed her mother's cell phone before she even exited the car. Her mother didn't pick up until Samantha stepped inside and shut the door behind her.

"Samantha." She sounded surprised. "Your dad and I are just opening the store. Is everything okay?"

Dispensing with the niceties, Samantha came straight to the point. "Did you tell Jeff where I live?"

"Was it supposed to be a secret?" her mother asked in an oh-so-innocent voice.

"You *did* tell him, and without even checking with me first? Without giving me advance warning? How dare you!"

"Calm down. You have the same email and cell phone number you've always had. Jeff was going to contact you anyway. Besides, as William's father, he deserves to see his son."

"After what he did? He cheated on me and broke William's heart! He's never paid a dime of child support, and the bills he saddled me with... Three years later, I'm still struggling to pay them off. Jeff left and never looked back. So no, he lost that privilege."

"That's all in the past, Samantha. Maybe he realizes what he gave up. If there's a chance you two could reconcile..."

Samantha's jaw dropped. "For the millionth time, I don't want Jeff back, and I doubt he wants me. He's married to Kayla now, remember? They live in some backwoods commune."

"You don't know that he's happy with her."

Why had she even tried to explain? Her mother didn't listen and never had. She only heard what she wanted to. Samantha gritted her teeth in frustration. "Drop it, Mom."

"Fine. But you will let Jeff see William." It was a statement, not a question.

"I need to think about that."

"No, you don't. For both Jeff's and William's sakes, you must."

She had a point. If Samantha prepped her son as to what to expect and stuck close by.... "I guess so," she grudgingly replied.

"Good girl."

"I'm not a girl, Mom. I'm a thirty-year-old woman."

"You know what I mean." After a lengthy silence, her mother said, "I don't know what else to say."

"How about, 'I'm sorry I told Jeff where to find you without first checking with you.'"

Of course, the exasperating woman failed to apologize. She never did.

"We're having a mid-winter sale, and customers are starting to trickle in," she said. "I should go. Let me know what happens with Jeff."

Grumbling, Samantha disconnected.

She thought about calling Adam. By now his shift had ended and he was visiting his father. Who knew why he was the one person she needed. Never mind— her pride wouldn't let her contact him.

She could use a friendly ear, someone she trusted. A call to Jana went to voicemail. No doubt her friend was swamped with the usual breakfast customers. Samantha left a message, asking her to call.

Gossip that Betty was, she knew all about Jeff, and as far as Samantha knew, she hadn't shared any of the details. Samantha assumed she could trust the woman on this, too. But her neighbor was still out of town. Samantha didn't feel comfortable confiding in anyone else.

What to do, what to do?

First on the list, protect William by making an appointment with the lawyer. Forget saving enough for the fee upfront. This was too important to put off.

Sending a silent thank-you to Adam for giving her Dwight Cornell's business card, she punched in his number.

BEFORE ADAM CLOCKED out Wednesday morning, he learned that his written exam had been scheduled for the following Wednesday, immediately after his shift ended. Which gave him one week to cram.

He didn't mind hitting the books day and night if it meant getting the thing over with. Next up, if he passed—no, *after* he passed—was the physical test, followed by a face-to-face interview before a panel of superiors.

He thought about telling his pop that the test had been scheduled, but decided to keep the information to himself for now.

He intended to drive home and hit the books. Instead, the 4Runner pulled up in front of Sam's place.

Hell if he knew what he was doing here. She didn't want him coming around.

Shaking his head, he killed the engine. He stayed in the car, fighting the urge to knock on the door.

Wait. Wasn't Betty out of town? Then Sam might even let him in. That or slam the door in his face.

From the car, he saw her through the kitchen window, pacing back and forth like a caged tigress. Even out here, he could sense the tension radiating from her.

Curiosity got the better of him. Before he knew it, he rang the bell. Without waiting for her to answer, he tried the latch. Unlocked. That wasn't like her.

Concerned, but not about to go in without her okay, he stuck his head inside. "Sam?" he called out warily.

"Adam!" From the kitchen, she hurried toward him. "Thank goodness you're here."

She seemed relieved to see him. Go figure. Her hair was every which way, and her normally pink cheeks pale.

Something was wrong. Adam shrugged out of his jacket and tossed it at the doorknob. "What happened?"

She chewed her lip, which explained why it looked red and sore. "I'm so upset. Come into the kitchen. That's where I left my phone."

She wasn't making any sense. Seriously worried, he followed her down the hall.

Her cell phone sat on the kitchen table. She poured herself a coffee and, without asking, filled him a mug. They took their usual seats. After she pressed a few buttons on the phone, she handed it to him. "Take a look at this email. It's from Jeff, my ex."

Adam read the message and frowned. "He's coming here."

"Yep. My darling mother told him where to find me."

"Nice of her," he muttered.

"She has some misguided belief that we're going to reconcile."

The thought of Sam with the man who'd hurt her and William ticked Adam off. Under the table, his hands fisted. "Do you want that?" he asked, careful to keep his tone neutral.

"Are you kidding? I'd rather have my arms chopped off."

He'd barely sucked in a relieved breath before she went on in a rush.

"I'm scared he wants to take William away from me."

Her eyes started to fill. *Uh-oh.* But she surprised him and blinked back the tears. She was tough, and he admired her for that.

"It's been what, three years since you heard from him?" Adam shook his head. "It wouldn't make sense for him to try and take William."

She plowed her fingers through her hair. "I can't imagine any other reason why, out of the blue, he's decided to come to Guff's Lake."

Adam had no idea. "This is probably a good time to get hold of Dwight Cornell."

"I did, just as soon as I hung up from bawling out my mother this morning. He's going to squeeze me into his schedule this afternoon."

"That's good."

"Except, I can't find anyone to watch William. I can't bring him with me. I called several of his school friends' moms, but no one can take him today. Betty is out of town, and Jana and everyone else I can think of is working. By the way, before Betty left, I told her you and I stopped seeing each other."

Adam nodded. He opened his mouth to ask Sam how she was doing otherwise, but something else came out. "I'll watch William for a few hours."

His own words surprised him. Had he really offered to babysit? He needed every second of his time off to study.

"I don't know, Adam. William still talks constantly about you."

"Then seeing me today won't make much difference. I won't encourage his feelings toward me. We'll hang out until you get back." She didn't look convinced. "You're in a bind. Let me do this for you."

She gave a resigned sigh. "All right. I'd planned to take him to see the horses this afternoon. Betty hired a man who stops by every morning to ride and care for them, but she invited us to stop by and visit with them any afternoon."

"I can take him over there."

"If you're sure. It isn't far, just across the field out back. My appointment is at two-thirty, so I should leave by two o'clock. I have no idea how long I'll be gone, but it could be a few hours. That's a long time to entertain a five-year-old boy."

Adam figured he could handle it. "We'll be okay."

Sam visibly relaxed. "You're a lifesaver."

Her grateful smile made him feel good, as if he'd walked into the sunshine. All too soon, the smile faded and her eyes narrowed a fraction.

"Why exactly did you stop by?" she asked.

If that wasn't the sixty-four-million-dollar question. "I thought you'd want to know I'll be taking my written exam a week from today. And, uh, I miss you."

"Really?" She sat back and crossed her arms. "I would never have guessed."

He shifted uncomfortably. "You're the one who decided we shouldn't see each other anymore."

"You could have called."

"What would be the point of that?"

Her lips suddenly compressed into a tight line. Wrong answer, Adam. Then she'd wanted him to call?

He would never understand women. Wishing he'd followed his own advice and driven straight home instead of coming here, he scrubbed his hand over his face. "What do you want, Sam?"

"The usual, world peace and an end to hunger and disease."

"What do you want from me?"

She hesitated then opened her mouth, and Adam braced for whatever she would say. But after a glance at the clock, she stood and collected the mugs. "I don't have time for this right now. I should run to the store before I pick up William."

"And I need to study for that test." Adam pushed to his feet. "I'll be back early this afternoon."

15

S eated in a plush chair in Dwight Cornell's hushed reception area, Samantha set aside the *People* magazine she'd picked up and checked her watch for the umpteenth time. She'd been waiting nearly twenty minutes. She appreciated that the attorney had squeezed her in, but for Adam's sake, she wished he would hurry up.

Adam wouldn't want to watch William for long. She hated burdening him with the responsibility in the first place, but she hadn't exactly had a choice. Without his help, she wouldn't be here now, and with Jeff arriving next week, she didn't have the luxury of postponing this appointment.

For those reasons, she was beyond grateful Adam had stopped by when she most needed him. The trouble was, talking and sitting across the kitchen table from him had felt all too right, as if it should always be this way between them.

He'd asked what she wanted from him. The unnerving answer had popped instantly into her mind.

She wanted him to love her and William.

Which only proved she was losing her mind. For starters, the timing was all wrong for love in her life.

As for Adam... The chances of his falling for her were about as likely as world peace.

The receptionist, a professional-looking woman about the same age as Samantha's mother, hung up from a call, rounded her gorgeous mahogany desk and approached Samantha. "Mr. Cornell wanted me to let you know he's just finishing up with a client. He should be out soon."

Relieved, Samantha texted Adam that she was running late.

No doubt William would be thrilled. He'd been overjoyed to see Adam, his grin lighting his up his whole face. Adam had been as friendly as always, but it was obvious that he regarded William as a nice little boy, period.

And now, Jeff was coming to town.

Although the temperature of the waiting area was comfortably warm, Samantha suddenly felt cold. Rubbing her arms didn't help because the chill came from inside her.

Down the hall, a door opened, and two men exited through it. One shrugged into his coat. The other, tall, graying at the temples and dressed in a suit, strode toward Samantha.

"You must be Ms. Everett," he said, smiling. "I'm Dwight Cornell."

His handshake was as firm as his direct gaze, and Samantha liked him at once. "Please call me Samantha. Thanks for seeing me on such short notice, Mr. Cornell."

"It's Dwight. You're lucky I had a last-minute cancellation."

He led her to an office every bit as luxurious as the reception area. Samantha wondered how much he charged and hoped what she needed from him wouldn't add too much to her debt load.

Never mind. William's well-being mattered far more than money.

The attorney gestured her to sit down across the desk, then took his own seat. "What can I do for you?"

He took notes as her story poured out—Jeff's infidelity, the divorce, the non-existent child support, and that now, after three years of silence and indifference, he suddenly wanted to see his son. "I don't know what he wants, or what to do," she finished.

"You've come to the right place," Dwight replied. "I can help you."

~

As ADAM and William entered the barn, the two stabled horses poked their heads out in curiosity and snorted.

"Cocoa is the brown horse, and Gordy is the other one," William said. "That's how they say, 'Hi.'"

Adam nodded. The old building felt surprisingly solid and comfortable, a snug buffer against the cold and damp.

The boy turned to the animals. "I brought my friend—Adam—today."

Relieved he understood they were just friends, Adam greeted the huge geldings. "Hey there, guys."

"I'll bet you missed me," William said.

They both seemed to nod, and Adam couldn't help but grin. "They sure are happy to see you, sport. Which one is your favorite?"

William leaned in, cupped his hand around his mouth, and whispered loudly. "Cocoa, but don't tell Gordy. I don't want to hurt his feelings."

Adam had always liked animals, but as a kid he'd never spared a thought for their feelings. Impressive that William did.

"Do you want to help me feed them their carrots?" William asked.

Clearly, he preferred to do the honors himself. Adam shook his head. "You go ahead. I'll sit on that hay bale against the wall and watch."

"That's where my mom likes to sit."

Adam settled back and imagined Sam beside him, smelling of vanilla and cinnamon and making him laugh.

He shook his head and told himself to knock it off. No way, no how.

William took his time, petting and murmuring and slowly doling out the dwindling supply of carrots, first to one horse and then the other.

That took awhile. Before long, Adam's mind wandered. Sam had texted that Dwight was running late, but surely by now, they'd met. If anyone could help her, the attorney could.

When William ran out of carrots, he climbed onto the hay bale and scooted close to Adam. Adam stretched his legs out in front of him and crossed them at the ankles. William attempted to do the same, only his feet didn't reach the ground by a long shot. It was kind of cute.

"Ever ridden a horse?" Adam asked.

"Uh-uh. Have you?"

"Nope. Do you want to learn?" William nodded, and Adam went on. "I'll bet if you asked, Mrs. Randall would give you a lesson."

"My mom will never let me do that."

"Why not?"

"She'll get scared that I'll fall and hurt myself."

Sam was pretty protective, all right. "It can't hurt to ask."

The boy grew visibly excited. "Do you think she might say yes?"

"If you don't try, you'll never know."

"Will you be there when I do?"

"Sure...if I'm around."

"Like when she comes home later?"

Adam had no idea whether Sam wanted him to stick around then, or if he even wanted to start up with her again. "Whether I'm there or not, give her a chance to hang up her coat and relax. Then you might have better luck."

"Okay." William screwed up his face in thought. "Today, everyone in this barn is a boy. No girls allowed."

"Hey, I like girls."

"Not me." William's little nose wrinkled.

"What about your mom?"

"She's not a girl, she's my mom."

Adam barely stifled his snort. "I see. When you're older, you'll change your mind about girls."

William scooted forward and swung his legs back and forth, kicking the hay with his heels. "I wish I could take Cocoa and Gordy home with me."

"You're out of luck there, sport, but you can come visit them any time you want." Adam's cell phone beeped, signaling a text. "I'll bet that's your mom." He checked the message. "She's on her way home. Ready to go?"

The boy nodded and slid to the ground. He waved at the horses. "See you later, crocodile."

Adam chuckled. "You mean 'alligator.' That way the words rhyme."

"What's a rhyme?" William asked as they ambled toward the barn door.

"When words make that the same sounds. Like 'later' and 'alligator.'" Outside, Adam started to close the door.

"No," William said. "My mom lets me do that."

Adam put his hands up and stepped back. "Have at it."

After much grunting and effort, William secured the latch.

"Good job," Adam said.

The boy seemed to stand taller. As they started across the field, he reached up for Adam's hand.

Cold, trusting little fingers clasped hold, and emotions Adam didn't understand crowded his chest. He coughed to clear his throat. "We're buddies, but that's all we are. Okay?"

William nodded somberly. "You're my very bestest friend, ever. Even better than Douglas and Harper."

What could Adam say to that? "I like you, too, sport."

By the time Samantha pulled up the driveway, the sun was slanting toward the horizon. Poor Adam must be anxious to leave. Expecting him to be waiting with jacket in hand, she entered the house. Instead, she found him at the kitchen table, flipping through a magazine, while William crawled around the floor with several of his racecars.

The picture of a peaceful father and his son. Except fatherhood wasn't even on Adam's radar. Samantha firmly pushed the thought away.

"Mom!" William jumped up to give her a hug.

"Hi! Did you and Adam have a good time?"

Her son gave an enthusiastic nod. "Cocoa and Gordy were happy to see me. I fed them all my carrots, and Adam sat on the hay and watched, just like you do. Adam let me latch the door, too, and I know what a rhyme is. It's when words have the same sounds, like —" he broke off and looked to Adam.

"Boy and toy," Adam said.

"Like that." William paused for a moment then added, "Adam says that someday I'll like girls. Blech."

The man's guilty-as-charged shrug and unrepentant grin had her shaking her head and smiling. "Did he?"

"Yeah." Nose wrinkled, William plunked onto the floor again and returned to his racecars.

"Did the meeting go okay?" Adam asked.

"Yes." Samantha didn't want to say anything more in front of her son. "We'll talk about that later."

William tugged on her pant leg. "Mom, I'm hungry."

"All right, I'll start dinner."

"Can Adam eat with us?" A pleading look filled his widened eyes.

Samantha hated to say no, but with her heart on the line, she couldn't handle that. Over her son's head, she met Adam's questioning gaze. He didn't seem keen to stay, either.

"I'm afraid not, sweetie. Adam's been here for a long time. He has a big test next week, and he needs to study."

"She's right." Adam ruffled William's hair. "I should get home."

"Wait, Adam!" William jumped up again. "Mom, are you relaxed and stuff?"

"I guess so," she said, confused. "Why?"

"'Cause Adam said to wait to ask until you are."

The firefighter glanced down and shook his head, making her curious. "Ask me what?"

"If I can ride Cocoa or Gordy."

"I don't know. I mean, they're big animals, and you're a little boy..."

"Not too little! Tell her, Adam."

"It's her decision, sport. But if it were me, I'd ask Mrs. Randall what she recommends."

"Will you talk to her, Mom? Will you?"

"She'll be gone for a couple more weeks, but the next time I see her, yes."

"All right!" Her son fist-bumped Adam.

"Listen, sport, I need to talk to your mom before I leave."

William nodded and glanced from Samantha to Adam.

"By ourselves," Adam said. "Take your cars into the living room and play with them there, okay?"

Her son left the room. "How did he do this afternoon?" she asked in a low voice.

"Just fine. You're raising a great kid."

"I try." She gave a proud smile. "I'm not sure about the horse riding thing."

"See what Mrs. Randall says. Tell me about the meeting."

"Thanks for referring me to Dwight. He's going to draw up a document asking Jeff to give up his parental rights in exchange for me not suing him for the back child support he owes. If I sue, Jeff will either have to pay me the money he owes or face jail time. He's never been good with money, and I'm guessing he doesn't have anything saved."

"Sound like a fair offer to me."

"Let's hope Jeff agrees. I just wish I knew what he

wants to talk to me about, and why he suddenly wants to see his son. I guess I'll find out."

Samantha shuddered at the very thought, but as Dwight had assured her, with a face-to-face meeting, she could hand him the relinquishment of parental rights document.

"Are you going to let him see William alone?"

"No way." She crossed her arms.

"Smart. When are you going to tell William that his dad is coming to visit?"

"Not until I have to. A few days before Jeff arrives."

Her face must have reflected her dread, for Adam gave her a sympathetic look. "You're in a tough spot. If you need me to stand beside you, just ask. What day is he coming?"

"He hasn't said yet. You've already done so much, Adam. This is something I need to do alone."

"All right. By the way, you'll be happy to know William considers us as friends and nothing more."

"That's a relief," Samantha said, hoping her son understood Adam would never be more than a friend. "Thanks again for helping me out today. I owe you, big-time."

"No problem."

They started toward the entry, stopping in the living room, and Samantha called out to her son. "Say good-bye to Adam, William."

He jumped up, ran to Adam, and threw his arms around his legs. "Bye! I had fun visiting the horses with you."

Adam patted his little shoulder awkwardly. "Back at ya, good buddy. Remember to do what your mom says."

The boy nodded before scampering back to his toys.

After shrugging into his jacket, Adam touched Samantha's cheek with his warm, roughened fingers. His eyes darkened irresistibly with heat. Hardly aware of her own actions, she started to lean into his touch.

No, she silently ordered. She ducked away. "Good luck with the studying."

"Good luck with your thing, too."

Will I see you again? The question hung foremost in her mind, but she wasn't going to ask.

To her disappointment, Adam said nothing more. He reached for the doorknob. As he stepped outside, a gust of cold air rushed in.

Shivering, Samantha shut the door. Then she returned to the kitchen to make dinner.

16

The email from Jeff, the appointment with the attorney, and the losing battle over her wayward feelings for Adam added up to an exhausting day. After tucking William in for the night, Samantha wanted to crawl into her own bed. And she would, as soon as she prepped for baking for the following morning. She was scooping flour into the bowl of the commercial mixer when Jana phoned.

"You called earlier. Sorry I couldn't get back to you until now. You sounded worried."

The mixing could wait. Samantha sank onto a kitchen chair. "You have no idea. The worst has happened. Jeff has decided to pay us a visit next week."

"No! I'm in shock."

"You and me both." Samantha filled her friend in. "I'm scared, Jana. What if he tries to take William away from me?"

"Then you text me immediately. I'll round up some of our men friends, and we'll take care of him."

Knowing Jana was looking out for her felt good, and Samantha blew out a breath. "I will. How are you?"

"Doing okay," Jana said. "Listen, I just found out

that Deb's grandson has strep throat. According to the pediatrician, he's contagious until he's been on antibiotics for twenty-four hours. That means his usual daycare is out, and Deb will be taking care of him tomorrow. Our knitting class has been cancelled."

"Well, shoot. I so needed the distraction."

"I'll bet. Speaking of distractions…. Does Adam know your ex is coming to town?"

"Yes, and he recommended a super attorney named Dwight Cornell. I met with him this afternoon, while Adam watched William."

"Adam babysat." Jana sounded incredulous.

"Only because I mentioned that I was desperate for a sitter when he stopped by."

"I'm confused. I thought you two decided not to see each other anymore."

"We did," Samantha said.

"Well, that's interesting. I know Dwight Cornell. He handled my sister's divorce. He's sharp, the best around. If he's helping you, you're in good hands."

Samantha agreed. Still, whatever happened depended on Jeff.

AFTER STUDYING MOST OF THURSDAY, Adam's brain was about to explode. Needing to work off his restless energy, he headed for Upton's, a gym he used when offduty, to meet Rafe at the racquetball court.

As they changed in the men's locker room, Rafe shook his head. "Sure you're up for this? 'Cause I'm gonna whup your ass all the way to Mexico."

Adam snorted. "Don't let these bloodshot eyes fool you. I may be studied out, but I'm ready to trounce your butt so bad, you won't even know what hit you."

"Why are you studying so much?" His buddy squinted at him. "You've been a firefighter for nine years. You sat through sixteen weeks of classes, never missing a single one, even when you screwed up your ankle and wrist. You already know most of what will be covered on that test. Hell, you probably don't even need to study."

"It pays to be prepared. Plus, there's a lot of stuff about management I didn't know until recently that I wanted to drum into my brain." Adam double-knotted his sneakers, then straightened. "Let's do this."

Some ninety minutes later, dripping sweat and feeling good, Adam pumped the air with his fist. "That's three out of five games to me. You owe me a pitcher."

Rafe grumbled good-naturedly.

After showering and changing, they wandered a few blocks east and crossed the street to Lucky Joe's. Even on a weeknight without live music, a lively crowd filled the place.

After ordering a pitcher and food at the bar, Adam and Rafe found a table in the back.

"I hear Sam's ex is coming to town," Rafe said.

"Bummer, huh? Who told you?"

"I stopped at General Hardware this morning to pick up spackle and paint for repairs on one of my rentals, and overheard two people in the checkout line mention it."

Sam had only found out yesterday, but news always traveled fast in Guff's Lake. Adam shook his head and wondered if she realized people were talking about her ex. She wouldn't like that.

"How'd you find out?" Rafe asked.

"From Sam. I watched her kid yesterday, while she met with Dwight Cornell."

"You watched Sam's son." Rafe's surprise was almost comical.

"She couldn't find anyone else, and she needed to see Dwight ASAP."

"So, she hit on you to babysit."

"Nope, I offered when I stopped over there." When his friend started to grin, Adam narrow-eyed him. "Do. Not. Ask."

"Whatever." Rafe put his hands up, but his grin lingered. "I thought Sam divorced before she moved here."

"About three years ago. Will you be at poker tomorrow night?"

"Go ahead, change the subject. Yeah, I'll be there. You?"

Adam was leaning against it. He didn't want to field any questions about Sam from the other guys. He shrugged. "Haven't decided."

The food and beer arrived, and he and Rafe dropped the conversation and slaked their hunger and thirst.

"It's good for a boy to see his father," Rafe commented after a while.

"You'd think. This guy has been AWOL since the divorce. It makes you wonder why he's suddenly taken an interest in a kid he doesn't even know anymore."

~

FOR WILLIAM'S SAKE, Samantha put on a happy face and hid the fact she was a nervous wreck about Jeff. Saturday he emailed that he would arrive Tuesday—exactly four days from now. So soon!

At the thought of telling William, her insides churned with dread. But he deserved to know.

She waited until the afternoon to break the news, when they were sitting at the kitchen table, sipping cocoa, and playing Candy Land during a sleeting rain.

"You won again!" After high-fiving her beaming son, she sucked in a fortifying breath and dove in. "I need to tell you something."

"That you don't want to play anymore?"

"You're right about that, but this isn't about Candy Land. It's about Jeff, your father." The man who had walked away from his own son didn't deserve to be referred to as Dad. "In a few days, he'll be coming to Guff's Lake to visit us."

William looked confused. "Why?"

Not about to lie, but working to tamp down her anxiety, Samantha spread out her hands. "He didn't say."

Her son reflected somberly on this before posing another question. "Does Jeff like racecars and horses and mutant ninja turtles?"

"I have no idea. You'll have to ask him."

"What does he look like?"

This she could answer. "Well, he's taller than I am, and thin. Or at least he was the last time I saw him. Let's clean up."

They returned the board and the game pieces to the box without William saying a word.

"Do you have any more questions?" Samantha asked before she stowed the game in the closet.

"Can I have more cocoa?"

Apparently, he didn't. She wasn't sure what to make of that. "It's 'May I.' And okay."

Wanting to leave the door open for whatever might bubble up in his mind, she smiled. "If there's anything else you want to know about Jeff, ask, okay?"

William nodded but didn't mention his father again, even when she tucked him into bed.

Relieved—for now, at least—she smoothed the covers and kissed him good night. She wasn't off the hook just yet. If her son had no questions now or over the next few days, he would when Jeff showed up.

Samantha didn't know what she dreaded more—Jeff's visit or the questions sure to arise.

17

W ith her son out cold until morning, Samantha could finally let down and stop pretending she wasn't freaked about Jeff's visit. Doing her usual Saturday night thing, she sprawled on the couch and relaxed with popcorn and a movie. Make that tried to relax. Thanks to her racing mind and frazzled nerves, she failed.

Her cell phone rang. *Adam*, the screen read.

Her heart lifted before she squelched her feelings. She'd been faking it about him, too, acting as if she didn't miss him.

She sat up, flipped off the TV, and did her best to sound nonchalant. "Adam...hi."

"Hey. Did you know people are talking about you and your ex?"

Samantha tensed into a giant ball of anxiety. "Great, just great. Thanks a lot, Jana."

"She wasn't supposed to say anything, huh?"

"I didn't exactly ask her to keep the visit to herself." If she had, her friend would never have breathed a word. "I'm so fed up with gossip about me and Jeff. One reason I left Enterprise was to get away from all that."

"In Guff's Lake? Ain't gonna happen." A faint rustling sound accompanied the words.

"Where are you?" Samantha asked.

"On the couch, channel-surfing."

"I'm doing the same thing, and eating popcorn." Although having lost her appetite, she'd barely tasted the stuff.

"Here, it's peanuts. Tell me, what are you wearing?"

"You don't want to know."

"I'm a guy, remember?"

"Since you asked...old sweats, with a grease stain on my shirt and a dried blob of jelly from where William grabbed my sleeve at breakfast this morning. There might also be a few chocolate smears on my pants."

"I'm so not getting turned on."

Hearing the smile in Adam's voice, Samantha laughed for the first time in days. "How's the studying going?"

"Let's just say the exam can't come soon enough."

"You sound burned out."

"Yep. I'm ready." More rustling. "I've been thinking about you."

"Really." Samantha set the popcorn bowl on the coffee table, stretched out on the couch, and stuck a throw pillow under her head. "What have you been thinking?"

"Wondering how you're doing."

"I'm hanging in there, keeping busy until Jeff comes and goes."

"Did you find out when that will be?"

"Tuesday afternoon."

"Change it to Thursday, when I'm off-shift and the

exam is behind me. Then if you need help, I can come straight over."

His offer meant a lot. "I want to get it over with as soon as possible. And as I said before, this is something I need to do by myself."

"You're sure?"

"I am. My plan is to be civil and calm, no matter what. I'm not going to mention the parental rights issue just yet."

"Saving it as your knockout punch. I like that. If anything goes wrong, call or text right away. Contact me regardless and let me know what happens."

"I will."

"What does William think about seeing his father?"

"I didn't get Jeff's email until this morning. I told William this afternoon. He hasn't said much, except to ask a few questions about Jeff's looks and whether he likes certain toys. By the way, we're both calling him 'Jeff.' He forfeited the right to be 'Dad.'"

With her own words, her fear ratcheted up. "What if he wants to make up for lost time?"

"Don't go there, Sam. Remember, you have a legal document he can't ignore."

"I know, but—"

"You could use a distraction right now. I can come over."

Adam's low growl of male interest washed over her, and for one aching moment, longing drowned out everything else. Her feelings were so strong that if she saw him tonight, she just might do something reckless and make love with him.

Which would definitely distract her, but not a good idea. "Better not."

"We could get down and dirty on the phone."

Samantha actually considered the suggestion before dismissing it. "Phone sex isn't my thing."

"I figured as much, but I'll bet the idea distracted you from your worries."

True. She smiled. "Good night, Adam."

"Night."

Feeling a little better, she headed upstairs for bed.

~

AFTER KINDERGARTEN TUESDAY, William seemed tense. Or maybe Samantha's own stress level had colored her perception.

They sat down for lunch.

"When is Jeff coming over?" William asked, picking at his sandwich.

She hated the anxious look on his face. "Sometime this afternoon. You love grilled cheese, but today you're not eating. Is something wrong with your food?"

"I'm not hungry."

She understood. Her own grilled cheese tasted like cardboard.

An hour passed, then another. She'd begun to wonder if Jeff would actually show up, when the doorbell rang.

"That's probably him," she said.

William pushed his chair back, stood, and dragged his feet toward the entry. "Check and make sure before you let him in," he told her.

Aw, he remembered. Despite a severe case of nerves, she gave him a fleeting smile. "Good idea."

She barely recognized the thin, bearded man with the shaggy hair standing at the door. The man she'd once considered handsome. "It's Jeff," she said. "Would you like to unlock the door?"

William shook his head. Samantha didn't blame him. She didn't want to let him in, either. *Civil and calm*, she reminded herself as she opened the door.

"Hello, Jeff." She couldn't summon another smile to save her life. "Come in."

"I go by 'Bodhi' now. It means *enlightened*." Leaving his shoes beside the welcome mat, he stepped inside.

William frowned. "I don't like beards."

Neither did Samantha, but her son needed a quick refresher on good manners. "That's not polite, William. What do you say to, um, Bodhi?"

The boy hung his head and kicked the toe of his shoe against the entry tile. "Sorry."

"It's all right."

Silence ticked by, thick and ominous.

Looking acutely uncomfortable, Bodhi tugged on his beard. He didn't seem to know what to do or say to William or her. He finally reached out to shake hands.

William looked taken aback and confused.

"Uh." Bodhi gave Samantha a helpless look. "I'm not sure how to talk to him."

If he hadn't deserted them, he wouldn't be struggling now, damn him. Anger Samantha thought she'd buried before the move to Guff's Lake reared up and seethed inside her, and she only avoided slapping his hairy face through sheer strength of will.

Civil and calm. Clasping her hands together at her waist, she forced a pleasant tone. "Start by addressing William directly instead of telling me."

Bodhi cleared his throat. "Hi, William."

"Hi."

"Why don't we sit down?" she suggested, gesturing toward the living room

Her hairy-faced ex perched stiffly on a chair. Samantha and William remained standing. Civility only went so far, and she refused to offer her ex refreshments.

"What grade are you in?" he asked without a trace of warmth.

He may as well have been meeting William for the first time. In a sense, he was. At two, William had barely been able to string three words together, let alone hold a conversation.

"Kindergarten. I go to Guff's Lake Elementary." Her son pointed at the orange lettering on his long-sleeve T-shirt.

Bodhi nodded. "At Peace Village, all children are home schooled."

He sounded smug, as if his community's way was superior to the Guff's Lake schools.

Samantha bit back a sarcastic retort. "Do you and Kayla have children?"

"She changed her name to Harmony. No, we don't."

Had Bodhi come because they wanted a son—her son? He wasn't exactly acting like a long-lost father, but that could be nerves.

Afraid all over again, Samantha stepped behind William and placed her hands on his shoulders.

"Ow, Mom. Don't squeeze me so hard."

She hadn't realized. Releasing her grip, she smoothed his T-shirt over his narrow shoulders. "Do you want to show, um, Bodhi your racecars?"

William shook his head.

"How about some of your other toys?"

He thought about that for a while. "I guess you can see my firefighter hat. Adam gave it to me."

"Who's Adam?"

"My bestest friend." William gave Bodhi a challenging look as if daring him to dispute the fact.

"Why don't you go and get the hat?" Samantha suggested, wanting to speak with her former husband privately. "It's on the ironing board in the basement, where you left it when you helped with the laundry."

As soon as William headed toward the basement steps, she eyed her ex. "Why are you here?" she asked in a voice too low to carry.

"Because I want to be an elder at Peace Village."

Okay. "What does that have to do with William and me?"

"Until I make amends for my past wrongs, I can't be considered for the position."

Was that all he wanted? What about William? Samantha narrowed her eyes. "How exactly do you plan to make amends?"

"With an apology."

"You could have just called and saved yourself the trip."

"Leader Aadi requires me to do it in person."

"Who?"

"Our founder. His name means, 'He who is most important.'"

When Samantha frowned, Bodhi went on. "I have three fathers—God above, my biological father, and Leader Aadi. As my spiritual guide, he is most important."

Samantha thought Jeff sadly misguided, but she didn't really care what he believed, as long they got down to business. Mentally crossing her fingers that once he did his apologizing, he would leave and never come back, she nodded. "Go ahead and say what you came here to say."

Bodhi pressed his hands together, prayer-like,

bowed his head, and murmured strange words before he began. "I shouldn't have made love with Harmony while you and I were still married. I shouldn't have turned my back on you and William. For these sins, I'm truly sorry."

He actually looked contrite, which counted for something. Still, if he expected to make amends for the pain he'd caused with one little "I'm sorry..."

Forget civil and calm. Hand on her hips, Samantha glared at him. "After what you pulled, you should be. You hurt William and me, left us broke and in debt, and never looked back. I'm still paying off the credit card debt for items you charged and took with you. So no, Jeff, your too-little, too-late apology won't cut it. It might help, though, if you reimburse me and pay off the remaining debt."

"It's Bodhi." Without another word, he glanced at the floor and remained silent. Nope, he wasn't going to reimburse her or assume his debt. That came as no surprise. But his next words did.

"Becoming an elder requires me to atone. But I also need forgiveness from you and William."

Samantha let out a hollow laugh. "On a cold day in hell."

Bodhi drew himself up straight. "Without your forgiveness I can't become an elder, and that is not acceptable. My spiritual growth depends on it."

He made the matter sound like life and death. All Samantha cared about was that he go back where he came from as soon as possible and never bother them again—after he signed the papers Dwight Cornell had drawn up. "Let me get this straight. If I forgive you, you'll go away?"

"It has to be both you and William. Then yes, I'll leave."

The idea that her son forgive what he didn't even understand chafed at her. "Be reasonable. He's only five years old. He doesn't know you except that you haven't been around."

"Then I expect we'll need to spend time together. I have no doubt that as he comes to know me, he will forgive me."

Hardly an appealing idea. She narrowed her eyes. "Exactly how long are you planning to stay in Guff's Lake?"

"As long as it takes."

Chills ran up her spine, and she fought to rein in her rising panic. "Don't you have to get back? What about Harmony?"

"She and Leader Aadi both understand how important this is."

What if his end goal was to slowly slip back into William's life and eventually convince her son to live with him and Kayla?

Samantha told herself to get a grip and be rational —that didn't seem like what he wanted—but her fear overpowered everything else.

So much so, she didn't dare step into her office, where she'd locked the parental rights document in the desk drawer. She simply didn't trust Bodhi enough to leave him alone in the house, especially with William alone in the basement.

Why hadn't she kept the papers within easy reach?

She crossed her arms to hide her trembling hands. "If you think you can take William away from me, think again."

Bodhi had the gall to look offended. "I would never do that, Samantha."

"And I should believe you why?"

"Because I give you my word."

She curled her lip. "That doesn't mean much to me."

"Why are you talking so loud, Mom?" William asked as he returned to the living room wearing his hat.

"I don't know, honey. I guess to make sure Bodhi heard what I said."

"You look like a firefighter in that hat, William," her ex said.

"It's pretend. Adam is a real firefighter."

Bodhi frowned. "I thought Adam was a little boy."

"No, he's a man, and he's my friend."

"Ah." A speculative look crossed Bodhi's face. He angled his chin at Samantha. "You and Adam are together."

She didn't miss her son's yearning look. He wanted the same thing she did—to have Adam in their lives permanently. It wasn't going to happen, not in the way they both wanted.

She shook her head. "We're friends, that's all."

William removed the hat and hugged it to his chest. "Mom, I want to take a nap."

Samantha's jaw dropped. He never asked to nap. "As long as it's a short one. Otherwise, you'll be up until midnight. Go on upstairs. I'll see Bodhi out and then come tuck you in."

As her son trudged toward the stairs, his biological father called out, "I'll be back tomorrow, William."

"I don't want you to come."

Samantha should have scolded him for his rudeness, but she agreed with him.

"He's not my friend, and I don't want him here," he repeated.

The man looked so crushed she actually felt sorry

for him. Which went to show what a basket case she was.

"We'll talk about this later," she told her son.

"What time should I come tomorrow?" Bodhi asked at the door.

Had he not heard William? Samantha shook her head. "Tomorrow won't work."

"I need to come back."

His lips thinned stubbornly, and she knew he wouldn't be put off for long. Just as well. She needed him to come back and sign the document relinquishing his parental rights. But William needed some time, and she would honor that.

"I'll text and let you know when. Bye." She all but pushed him out the door.

amantha found her son sitting on the bedroom floor, looking at a book. "I thought you wanted to take a nap."

"I'm not tired. Mom, I don't like Bodhi. You don't like him, either."

She'd never known William to hide in his room in order to get away from someone. Shocked but understanding, she sank down beside him.

"You're right. But without him, you wouldn't be here."

"I still don't want him for my dad. I want Adam,"

The words caught her totally off-guard, especially coming on the heels of Bhodi's visit. She put her arm around her son. "Adam's a great guy, for sure. But for him to be your dad, he and I would have to love each other and get married."

"Why don't you love each other?"

Oh, she was definitely on the verge of loving Adam, but the feeling was not mutual. She managed a smile. "That's just how things go sometimes. We like each other a lot, though."

"Adam really likes me."

"That's true. Now, about Bhodi He won't be in

town too long, but you heard him say that while he's here, he wants to see you again."

"Do I have to?"

"Yes. Not tomorrow, but how about the day after?"

"Then will he go away?"

"That's what I'm hoping."

Samantha silently vowed to do everything possible to make Bhodi "go away." If things went as they should, the legal document she gave him would do the trick.

BETWEEN AN APARTMENT FIRE, a couple of false alarms, and reviewing stuff he already knew cold for the exam, Adam spent a reasonably busy Tuesday. During the lulls between calls, while he worked out in the gym and helped prep the fire engine for the next call, he thought about Sam and William and her ex. She knew how to be tough, and could take care of herself.

But picturing her ex in the house, talking to her, looking at her... That made him nuts.

By dinner, he was close to losing it, and the captain and his crewmates knew it. They didn't even razz him about his test tomorrow or his feelings for Sam.

On cleanup duty after the meal, he was clearing platters from the table when his cell phone pinged, signaling a text.

"It's from Sam," he said, relieved to finally hear from her.

"Go ahead and phone her," Rafe offered. "I'll take over cleanup. You do it for me next time."

"No need. She's going to call after William falls asleep."

When the kitchen was spick and span and the rest

of the evening chores done, Adam checked his watch. William's bedtime had come and gone, and any minute now, he'd hear from Sam. For privacy, he stepped out front, into the crisp, clear night.

As he headed out to walk around the well-lit building, his cell phone rang. "Hey." Keen to get to the nitty-gritty, he didn't wait for a greeting. "And?"

"It was pretty awful."

If her ex had laid even a finger on her... Adam stiffened. "Tell me."

"Take it easy. He didn't hurt me."

Adam rolled his shoulders. "For his sake, that's good."

"You should have seen him. Too thin, with long hair and a bushy beard. He looked like a bum in clean clothes."

"I'll bet William liked that."

"Not at all. He didn't like Bodhi at all. That's the name he goes by now."

"Interesting. Did he say what he wanted?"

"Yes. At least he waited 'til William was out of hearing range. He's here to, and I quote, 'atone for his sins,' so that he can become an elder at Peace Village."

Adam frowned. "I don't follow."

"You're out of breath."

Adam realized he was moving at quite a clip. Chalk that up to stress. "I'm walking around the building. Atoning for his sins?"

"According to Bhodi, atoning means apologizing to William and me. Apparently, the head guy at Peace Village insisted he do that in person."

"Did he apologize?"

"He said he was sorry for cheating on me with Kayla, who, by the way, changed her name to 'Harmony,' and for walking out the way he did." She sniffed.

"As if one apology makes up for anything. I lost my cool."

Adam wished he could have seen that. "Yeah?"

"I told him off, and suggested that if he wanted to pay me back and finish paying off the rest of the debt he saddled me with, I might be more agreeable. Of course, he ignored the idea. That's when I got scared."

Stopping mid-stride, Adam tensed. "Did he threaten you?"

"Not outright. Bhodi believes that becoming an elder at his commune will help him on his spiritual path. Don't ask me why because I have no idea. Becoming an elder requires him to atone, but he also needs both me and William to forgive him."

"Forgiveness from a little kid?" Adam frowned into the darkness.

"Exactly my reaction."

"Are you going to forgive him?"

"Never." Her voice rang with conviction.

Adam understood. He also knew holding onto blame could cause heavy damage to the person doing the blaming. Just look at the old man. Hell, look at his own self. "That'd be hard, all right."

"I sense a 'but.'"

"I'm not saying you should forgive him, only that it might help if you did."

"Do you want to hear what happened or not?"

Looked as if forgiveness was off the table. "Go on."

"Bhodi intends to stay in Guff's Lake for as long as it takes him to earn our forgiveness."

No wonder she was scared. "I don't like that at all."

She swallowed audibly. "The thing is, he and Kayla don't have children, and...and I think his end goal is to get William comfortable with him, and then take him to Peace Village, so he and Kayla can raise him."

"He said that?"

"He actually promised the opposite, that he would never try to take William from me. But I don't trust him."

With Bhodi's track record, Adam didn't blame her. "William would never want to leave you, Sam. You're his mother," he reasoned. "And remember, you have Dwight Cornell on your side, and probably any court of law in the country. Bhodi would never be able to take William from you."

"So I keep assuring myself, and yet... If you could have seen and heard him... I can't help but worry."

Adam swore. "You showed him the legal form, right?"

"I assumed I wouldn't need it today. I didn't have it nearby, and I was uncomfortable leaving the room to get it. Then William came back, and Bhodi and I couldn't talk anymore. I'll give it to him next time I see him."

"Which is when?"

"He asked to visit again tomorrow, only William didn't want him here. I'm thinking Thursday. I'll invite him to come while William is in kindergarten so we can talk. I'll give him the document then. Which reminds me, I need to let Jana know I'll be skipping this week's knitting class."

"You also might want to check in with Dwight."

"If I feel the need, I will. By the way, your name came up when William showed Bhodi his firefighter hat."

Adam wasn't sure why that pleased him. "He mentioned me?"

"Yes, and now Bhodi thinks you and I are together."

She paused, and Adam figured he should say

something. He scratched his head and tried to come up with a comment, but Sam beat him to it.

"I explained that you and I are friends."

He couldn't figure a response to that, either.

She hurried on, as if she wanted to fill in the awkward silence between them. "Then, later, William... Never mind."

"What?"

"It's nothing. Now, you know what happened."

"I appreciate you filling me in. You going to be able to sleep tonight?"

"I'd better. I'm exhausted. You?"

"That's the plan, unless we get a bunch of calls."

"For your sake, let it be a quiet night. You need to be rested when you take the test tomorrow. You're going to ace that thing."

"From your mouth to God's ears."

19

As soon as Samantha finished prepping the kitchen for the morning baking Wednesday night, she reached for her cell phone. She wanted to update Jana on the latest, and also get some reassurance. With Bhodi due back in the morning, she needed the support. As she accessed her friend's number, the doorbell rang. She was so jittery she dropped her cell phone.

Outside, the motion lights blazed through the darkness. Through the peephole she saw Adam. She hadn't heard from him today, but he'd been busy with his exam.

Oh, it was good to see him. She held the door open with a welcoming smile. "You must have survived the test. You're alive."

"Barely. But it's over." Inside, he hung his jacket on the doorknob.

Samantha opened her mouth to ask if he thought he'd passed, when he stepped in close and kissed her. The question faded from her mind.

Relishing the feel of his strong arms around her, and wanting to forget her troubles for a little while, she lost herself in sensations—Adam's spicy aftershave and masculine scent, his hard, warm body and attentive lips. She melted on the spot, growing limp with desire and aching for more.

All too soon, he released her.

"I've been thinking about that since I finished the exam," he said. "Now I'm good."

Samantha felt better, too. "Can I get you a beer or a glass of wine?"

He shook his head. "Alcohol would put me to sleep. Let's sit."

They settled on the couch, his arm circling her shoulders. Samantha couldn't help but snuggle into his side. "Tell me about the test."

"It wasn't easy, and took me several hours." Looking exhausted, he scrubbed a weary hand over his face.

"When will you know if you passed?"

"In a couple of days. Next comes the physical, and then, if things fall into place the way they should, the head honchos will contact me in for an interview."

"I'll be rooting for you."

"Thanks. Bhodi comes again tomorrow, right?"

"Like it or not." She sighed. "He agreed that we should talk while William is in kindergarten. This time, I'll be ready with the legal paper in hand. Once he signs and has it notarized, he can bring it back, see William, and say good-bye. At least that's the plan."

"If he doesn't want to fork out a lot money or go to jail, signing and leaving are his only alternatives." Adam cupped her nape. "You're super tense."

"I can't help that. I doubt I'll be able to relax until I have Bhodi's notarized signature on that document."

"Too much tension is bad for you. I can help. Turn around."

She moved so her back was to him. Slowly, he

massaged her nape, shoulders, and lower back, spreading lovely heat wherever he touched.

"Ditch that shirt and bra and I'll do a more thorough job," he said.

Glancing at him over her shoulder, she widened her eyes. "Why, Mr. Healey, are you trying to seduce me?"

"I might be. It's been a while since we fooled around. Way too long."

Samantha agreed. While her common sense did battle with her hunger, Adam made room for her to stretch out on the couch.

"Lie down and get comfy." He flipped off the reading lamp.

Samantha hadn't bothered with a fire tonight, and light from the entry bathed the room in soft shadow. She removed her shirt and her bra, then lay on her stomach.

Using the coffee table as his seat, Adam worked at the knots in her shoulders, dissolving the kinks one by one, until her muscles relaxed and she felt like melted butter. She moaned. "That feels really good."

"So will this."

He slid his hands to her breasts, but her nipples pressed against the cushion. Burning for his touch, she whispered, "Let me turn over."

Once she was on her back, Adam did all the things she enjoyed, licking and sucking and stroking.

She was restless and aching for more, when he broke off and pulled her to a sitting position.

"I want you, Sam." His smoldering gaze combed over her swollen breasts, making her feel sexy and desired. "If we keep on like this, I won't be able to stop, and we will make love."

Wanting to be with him in that most intimate way, she nodded.

"Know that I can't make you any promises. Are you okay with that?"

She shouldn't be, but she wanted him so much—too much to push him away. "I'm not asking for promises," she said. "But there is a problem. I'm not on the pill, and I don't have any protection."

His eyes darkened. "Is that a 'yes?'"

"Not without protection."

The corners of his mouth lifted. "It just so happens I have a condom or two in my pocket."

"You planned this." She crossed her arms and slanted him a look.

He gave an unapologetic grin. "It pays to be prepared. Let's go to bed." He drew her to her feet and then tugged her toward the stairs.

Her bedroom stood at the opposite end of the hall from William's. As soon as they crossed the threshold, Adam shut and locked the door. Samantha had closed the curtains and removed the spread earlier.

Digging into his hip pocket, he pulled out several foil packets and he tossed them onto the nightstand. Next, he shrugged out of his shirt, and kicked off his shoes.

"Come here," he directed in the gruff, aroused voice that set off tremors inside her.

Without hesitation, Samantha complied. Bare breasts against bare chest—heaven.

Adam groaned and held her for a moment before capturing her mouth in a passionate kiss. "Let's get naked," he murmured against her lips.

Breathing hard, they shed their jeans.

Adam had seen Samantha naked before, but she'd never seen him. His powerful thighs and muscled legs were every bit as gorgeous and fit as his torso. His erection tented the fabric of his gray boxers.

Feeling sexy and daring, she knelt in front of him and pulled the boxers down and off. He was huge and glorious. She stroked the velvet skin of his shaft and then took him into her mouth.

Before long, he jerked and pulled her to her feet. "I'm near the edge, and I don't want to lose control until I'm deep inside you."

Ready for exactly that, Samantha reached for his hand. "Come to bed."

Moments later, the mattress dipped slightly under their combined weight. Adam kissed her thoroughly and slowly made his way down her body, each lick and stroke taking her higher.

Hot hands slid up her inner thighs, followed by open-mouth kisses. The part of her that most wanted him began to pulse.

He took his time getting there, until she was half out of her mind. "Please, Adam," she begged.

"Yes, ma'am." He put his mouth right there.

She almost went up in flames. She wanted to let go but not without him. She pulled on his ears, forcing him to stop.

"No, Adam. Like you, I want us to climax together."

"We will, after I finish what I'm doing."

Keeping a firm hold on his ears, she shook her head. "I want you inside me, now."

"Yes, Ma'am." He turned away and quickly sheathed himself. When he returned to her, he covered her with his body and slid inside.

Samantha closed her eyes. "Oh, dear God."

Supporting his weight on his arms, he raised up. "Sorry, Sam. I meant to ease in slowly, so you could adjust. But I'm too turned on."

"You did it just right. I just..." So aroused she could barely form the words, she paused. "You feel good."

Then there were no words at all, only sensations. Adam, so deep inside he became a part of her. Pulling almost all the way out, driving her mad. In deep again.

She felt the corded muscles in his back, the strain in his arms, and knew he fought to hold himself in check, waiting for her.

She loved him for that. Loved him, period, but she wasn't going to think about that now.

He teased her toward the edge, the tension inside coiling and tightening and pulsing. In and out, in and out, faster and faster, until the world blurred and faded away.

On a frantic wave of pleasure, she exploded. Adam growled and came with her.

When she drifted back to earth sometime later, she lay cradled against his side.

"You're not keyed up anymore," he teased, nuzzling the sensitive place under her ear.

Sated and relaxed, she smiled drowsily. "I can't even remember what that feels like."

"This was definitely worth waiting for." Adam kissed the top of her head then tipped up her chin and brushed his mouth over hers.

With an exhale of pure satisfaction, he collapsed against the pillow. Before long, his breathing evened out in sleep.

Samantha kissed his chest. His hand tightened possessively on her hip. She felt whole and content. And head over heels for the man beside her.

But Adam didn't want her love.

The glow inside her dimmed and her heart contracted painfully, a tiny preview of the hurt yet to come. For her own good and her own self-respect, she needed to get up and send him home.

She attempted to do exactly that.

"Where are you going?" he mumbled, wrapping his arms around her and pulling her back down.

How could she argue, when lying beside him was exactly where she wanted to be? Where she belonged? Tonight, anyway.

Self-respect be damned. "I'm not going anywhere."

She returned to his side. Determined to sleep, she closed her eyes.

The one saving grace was Adam would never know her true feelings. That was her last thought before she drifted off.

20

At three a.m., Adam woke to a blaring alarm clock. It was pitch dark and he was wrapped around Sam, spoon-style. She didn't so much as stir. Reaching across her, he silenced the alarm.

His groin pressed her soft skin. Instantly, he was hard. They'd made love twice, the second time even better than the first. What a shame they didn't have time for round three.

He untangled his legs from hers, then clicked on the reading lamp. "The alarm just went off. Time to rise and shine."

Her eyelids blinked open. "Already?"

"Afraid so. Your work hours suck worse than mine."

Yawning, she sat up, bringing the bed sheet with her. "I need to shower. I won't wake William for a couple of hours yet, so if you want to go back to sleep..."

Adam shook his head. "I should get going. I'll get up in a few minutes."

As Sam grabbed clean clothes from the dresser and hurried into the bathroom the sheet slipped, giving him a view of her great ass.

Hands propped under his head, he stared at the ceiling. Last night ranked up there as probably the best sex of his life. Then waking up with Sam nice and close... He liked that, too. Liked her, period.

A lot. Too much.

He was not falling for her, he assured himself. Credit the dynamite chemistry for making him feel so great. With Sam on the same page, life seemed pretty damn perfect.

The hiss of the shower called to him, and he considered joining her. But you didn't rush hot shower sex, and she was in a hurry.

Another time, then.

The water shut off. Not long after, she came out fully dressed and looked a lot more alert.

"You're quick," he said.

"I have too much to do to waste a second in the bathroom. There are clean towels in the bathroom closet. I'll see you downstairs."

She seemed a little distant, barely sparing him a glance. Adam chalked that up to the ton of work ahead of her, on top of worries about today's meeting with her ex.

Deciding to shower at home, he dressed and headed silently down the stairs. As he crossed the living room on his way to the kitchen, he noted that Sam had picked up last night's discarded clothing and fluffed the throw pillows. The room looked the same as when he'd arrived, as if things had never gotten hot and heavy.

Clangs and bangs sounded from the kitchen. Adam found Sam decked out in a bib apron and a hairnet. Hard at work, she spooned batter into muffin tins with quick precision.

"You don't look half-bad in a hairnet," he teased.

"But I like you better without it."

Without cracking a smile or glancing up from her task, she gestured at the gurgling coffee maker. "I'm afraid the coffee isn't ready yet."

She didn't ask him to stay and wait, but that was okay. Adam didn't want to get in her way.

"I need a shower and a shave. I'll get my caffeine fix later. How are you feeling about seeing your ex?"

"I'm sure it will be fine."

He nodded. "Thanks for last night. I enjoyed it...a lot."

She left off filling muffin tins and finally met his gaze. "Me, too."

Her gaze softened with something that looked dangerously close to love.

And here he'd thought they were of the same mind. He shoved his hands in his pockets. "You don't want to be falling for me, Sam. I'm a bad bet."

"Falling for you?" Up went her chin. "Where did you get that idea?"

He shrugged. "Just a feeling."

"You're mistaken. As I said last night, I don't expect any promises. But I have rethought what we did. It probably shouldn't happen again."

Dumbfounded, he eyed her. "Can we talk about this?"

"I'm a little busy right now." She slid the tins into the oven. "Would you mind letting yourself out?"

Well, hell. "No problem. Good luck with your ex."

Adam headed for the door, wishing he could erase the last few minutes and redo the conversation. Sure, he'd warned her not to fall for him for her own good, but between baking and her ex, she had enough on her mind. His timing sucked, and he felt like a total jackass.

He needed to straighten out this mess, and he drove away deep in thought. Moments later, he knew exactly how to do that.

~

THE SECOND SAMANTHA heard the door click shut behind Adam, she sank into a chair. She'd pulled it off, convinced him she didn't love him. When the opposite was true.

She wanted to have a good cry, but at the moment, she didn't have the time.

On the drive home from dropping William at kindergarten, she called Jana, using her Bluetooth. "Are you on your way to knitting?"

"Not quite. You'll be missed. We're all pulling for you."

How could they possibly know about Adam? Then Samantha realized her friend meant Bhodi "I appreciate the support."

"You don't sound so good. Are you worried?"

"A little. Cross your fingers Jeff isn't too upset when I ask him to give up his parental rights."

"Already crossed. Remember, if you need backup, there are lots of people ready and willing to step in."

"I'll keep that in mind. You want to hear something that has nothing to do with my ex? You have to swear you won't tell a soul."

"My lips are sealed."

Reassured, Samantha went on. "Adam stayed over last night."

"Lucky you," her friend replied. "As I keep saying, that man likes you a lot."

"Key word 'likes.'" Samantha couldn't stop a heavy sigh.

"Ah. You're in love with him."

"I so am."

"Does he know?"

"No. He thinks I don't want to get serious, either. That's what I told him when we talked about it earlier. When I believed it."

Jana made a sympathetic sound.

"There's more," Samantha added. "When William and I were talking about Bhodi yesterday, he flat-out said he wanted Adam to be his dad."

"Aw, he's in love, too. I'll bet Adam flipped out when he heard that."

"William said it when he wasn't around, thank goodness." Samantha turned onto her street. "Did I do the right thing, Jana?"

"You're asking me, the woman whose relationships never last more than six weeks?"

"I could use your advice."

"Well... If it was me standing in your shoes, I'd let what happens, happen, and enjoy the ride while it lasts."

"I'm not wired that way."

"I figured as much, but you asked. You never know, Adam just might fall for you, too."

Samantha doubted that. She pulled into the driveway. "I need to run. Bhodi will be here in half an hour. Think good thoughts."

"I will. Keep me posted."

Samantha had barely hung up her coat when the doorbell rang. She almost jumped out of her skin.

Bhodi had arrived early, and the papers were still locked in the desk drawer.

Out of habit, she squinted through the peephole. Not Bhodi Adam.

Why had he had come back?

21

S am opened the door without a trace of a smile. "Did you forget something?"

Ready to make things right, Adam went straight to the point. "I'm here to support you when your ex comes over."

"I don't need your support. I'll be fine."

"I'm sure you will, but I'm sticking around anyway." In case she needed him.

Muttering something about his stubborn streak, she blew her bangs out of her eyes. "All right, come in. I expect Bodhi any minute now, and I need to get the parental rights document from the desk in my office."

"What's the plan for this morning?" Adam followed her into a small room tucked onto the back of the house.

She unlocked the middle desk drawer and pulled out a large envelope. "I'll give this to Bodhi and ask him to bring it back signed and notarized this afternoon, so he can say good-bye to William."

The doorbell chimed.

"That's him." Her whole body stiffened. She sucked in a breath and exhaled loudly. "Here we go."

She squared her shoulders and headed for the

door, Adam staying at her side. Seconds later, he stood face-to-face with the man she'd once called her husband.

Her description of him had been dead on. Thin, a couple inches shorter than Adam, and a whole lot hairier, he could have passed as a harmless bum in clean clothes. Except for those eyes. Clear and alert, and yet somehow off.

The back of Adam's neck prickled. "Adam Healey," he said, extending his arm.

The other man did not shake his hand. "I'm Bodhi." He glanced at Sam. "I thought you wanted to talk privately."

Adam put his arm around her shoulders. "Just pretend I'm not here."

Her ex scowled. "What's this about, Samantha?"

"I had my lawyer draw up a legal agreement." Sam held out the envelope. "I'd like you to read through it, sign in front of a notary, and bring it back this afternoon."

Paying no attention to the envelope, Bodhi waved his hand in a dismissive gesture. "I no longer believe in legal documents."

Adam kept his arm around Sam. "If I were you, I'd believe in this one. You'd best give it a read."

Sam nodded. "It asks you to give up your parental rights in exchange for immunity from a lawsuit for the back child support you owe William and me. And you owe quite a bit. The amount is spelled out in the second paragraph of page two."

Once more she attempted to hand Bodhi the envelope. Again, he ignored her outstretched arm.

"I can't pay you," he said, shrugging. "Peace Village is mostly a barter economy. When a person needs something, we trade for it. If I do get paid, everything I earn goes into a community fund for emergencies. What I'm saying is, I don't have the money."

Adam wondered if the community fund covered the costs of the trip to Guff's Lake and hanging around. "Suit yourself. But if you can't pay and you don't sign, you're going to jail."

Bodhi's nose and forehead flushed red and he spewed out a stream of four-letter words that even Adam found offensive. "Watch your mouth," he warned, pulling Sam closer.

After a tense moment, the man bowed his head as if praying and murmured strange-sounding words. To Adam's relief, when he looked up, he seemed calmer.

"I came here to make amends and gain forgiveness, not fight. I don't need your boyfriend here for that, Samantha. He should leave."

"Not a chance." Holding tight to Sam, Adam opened the door. "Get out, before I lose my temper."

Sam cleared her throat. "You can say good-bye to William when you bring the document back later. In the meantime, read through it. Then find a notary and have your signature notarized—using your legal name, not Bodhi."

When the man still hesitated, Adam shoved the envelope at him. "Take. It. And do as Sam said."

Anger sparked in Bodhi's eyes and his lips thinned, but he accepted the envelope.

As soon as the door shut behind him, Sam's shoulders sagged. "That was scary. I'm glad you were here, Adam."

So was he. "You did fine, babe." He pulled her into a hug and kissed the top of her head.

After a moment, she moved out of his grasp. "What if he doesn't come back?"

Her eyes filled with shadows he hated to see.

"Have faith. If he doesn't show or comes back without having signed the document, follow through and sue his ass. I think I'll hang around awhile longer."

This time, she didn't argue.

She checked her watch. "I need to pick up William."

"You do that, and I'll fix lunch. I'll bet you didn't know I make a mean sandwich."

"I bought groceries yesterday, and the fridge is full. Use whatever you want. What am I going to tell William about why you're here?"

"Say that I felt like having lunch together."

SAMANTHA BARELY PULLED to a stop beside the 4Runner before William unbuckled his seatbelt, opened the door, and shot up the porch steps. By the time she caught up with him, he'd slipped through the door.

"Adam!" he called out, racing toward the kitchen.

His obvious joy and his big hug around the fire-fighter's waist made her heart hurt, but there was nothing she could do to protect herself, let alone her son.

Chuckling, Adam gave William a one-arm hug. "How ya doing, sport?"

"Good."

"School okay?"

"Uh-huh."

"Adam made sandwiches," Samantha pointed out. "Go wash up."

William ran toward the powder room. She filled a glass with milk and added a pitcher of ice water to the table.

Her son returned, carrying the firefighter hat.

"Please leave it on the spare chair until after lunch," she said.

For once, he didn't argue. After setting the hat down, he kicked at the floor and made a face. "Mom says Bodhi is coming over this afternoon."

"So I heard."

William slanted his head. "Do you know him?"

"We met earlier."

"He's my dad, but I don't like him."

Samantha sucked in a breath and mentally crossed her fingers William didn't ask Adam to fill that honor. He didn't, and the tension in her stomach eased a little.

"Let's sit down and eat." She shepherded her son to his chair.

"Will you be here when Bodhi comes?" William asked.

"You bet."

Adam's reassuring nod eased her raw nerves. Despite the way they'd left things this morning, she appreciated his support more than she could say. Her feelings for him had only deepened to the point that she wasn't at all sure she could hide them anymore. But she couldn't worry about that now.

"You need to eat," he reminded her. "Try the sandwich."

Having barely eaten at breakfast, she should have been famished. But misgivings as to whether Bhodi would come back with the signed document had killed any appetite. All the same, she tasted the sandwich. Adam hadn't exaggerated about his skills, and she managed to swallow a few bites.

William had no such problems. He was polishing off the last of his food when the doorbell chimed.

Samantha had begun to dread that sound. "There's Bhodi." She stood and carried her plate to the sink.

"Can I stay in here?" William asked, hugging his firefighter hat.

"For now, but when I call you, you have to come. All right?"

He nodded.

Adam accompanied her to the door, making her feel safe. "Come in," she said.

He gave Adam a wary look. "Don't believe I will. Here." He thrust the envelope at her. "It's signed and notarized."

She didn't have to force a pleased smile. "Thank you."

"Where's William?"

"In the kitchen. If you're not going to come in, he'll need his coat. I'll be right back."

Minutes later, she led her son onto the porch, where Adam waited with Bodhi. Neither man looked happy.

Samantha's ex glared at Adam. "Give us some space, man."

"I'll stay up here on the porch and keep an eye on things," Adam replied, his mild tone edged in steel.

Bodhi gestured at William. "Let's go down to the yard."

Unwilling to leave her son with him, Samantha grasped his small hand. "I'll come with you."

In the wintry brown grass beside the driveway, Bhodi hunkered down to William's level. "I'm sorry for the pain I've caused you, William. You're a nice boy, and you don't deserve that." At the moment, he sounded like a normal guy. "Will you forgive me?"

William looked to Samantha and frowned. "What does he mean, Mom?"

"He's apologizing for hurting you."

"I'm not hurt. I don't have any owies or Band-Aids."

"For hurting your feelings," she clarified.

His little brow wrinkled while he considered that. "Like when I say something mean and you get mad at me? And then I say I'm sorry, and you forgive me?"

"Yes, like that."

"Okay, Bodhi. I forgive you."

Her ex closed his eyes. When he opened them again, he straightened and faced Samantha. "Now you."

"I'm going to leave the past in the past and move on."

"Why can't you say that you forgive me?"

She couldn't lie. "Because it wouldn't be true."

The sudden dark flash in his eyes scared her. With an ominous scowl, Adam started down the steps.

Her ex-husband blinked, then once again became calm and rational. "I guess that'll have to be good enough."

He climbed into his car and backed out of the driveway.

Samantha sagged in relief. It was over.

22

A s Bodhi's car disappeared down the street, Adam glanced at Samantha with a concerned expression. "You okay?"

"Now that I have the signed papers and he's gone, I am."

"I thought the meeting went real well. Now that it's behind us, I could use a cup of coffee. We should talk. Privately."

He pinned her with a look that left little doubt what was on his mind. Their early morning conversation.

Given her strong feelings for him, that was probably a bad idea. But he'd stood by her today, and she owed him. Reluctantly, she agreed.

"William, I need to speak with Adam. It's such a pretty afternoon. Why don't you play outside for a while?"

"Do I have to? It's cold."

In a down jacket, hat, and mittens, he'd stay toasty warm. "Would you rather take a nap instead?" she asked.

"No nap!" He scrunched up his face, reminding

her of when she made him eat his vegetables. "Can I play in the backyard?"

"Of course. Adam and I will be in the kitchen. When you're ready to come in, use the back door."

"In case I don't see you later, bye, sport." Adam squeezed the boy's shoulder.

"Bye, Adam."

William broke into a run, laughing before he even rounded the house.

"He doesn't seem one bit confused or upset about Bodhi," she commented as she started a pot of coffee in the kitchen.

Adam got out the mugs. "I noticed. Your ex mellowed out quite a bit this afternoon. I'm sure that made the whole scene easier on William."

"Because you were there. I'll never be able to thank you enough."

"No thanks needed. You were strong and tough, and didn't lose your cool. I'm impressed."

The admiration in his eyes warmed her. Feeling brave and proud of herself, she stood a little taller and smiled.

"There's the pretty smile I've been waiting for," he said. "The one I wanted to see before I left early this morning. I don't like the way we left things."

He cared about her, really cared. Was there a chance he loved her? Samantha's heart swelled with the possibility.

Until she reminded herself not to get her hopes up. Adam didn't want love.

Two months ago, neither had she. But now... Afraid of betraying her feelings, she lowered her gaze.

"Hey." He tipped up her chin, forcing her to look at him. "I'm no good at reading minds. Talk to me."

The tenderness in his clear-blue eyes made anything but honesty impossible. She would tell him the truth—even if it meant never seeing him again.

"The coffee's ready," she managed around her suddenly dry throat. "Let's fill our cups and sit down. Then I'll explain."

~

SAM PERCHED STIFFLY across from Adam, her hands in a death grip around her mug, and Adam figured he wasn't going to like what he heard.

"The last two months have been..." She hesitated and started over. "I really appreciate everything you've done for William and me. Especially today."

Her words sounded an awful lot like good-bye. She was dumping him. Hell. His chest constricted. "Just say what you need to say."

She nodded. "I don't believe you're a bad bet, Adam Healey. I think you're a great guy."

Strangest breakup words ever. He eyed her warily. "There are plenty who would disagree."

"Such as?"

"My ex-wife, ex-girlfriends. My father."

"They're all mistaken. Every day, you risk your own safety to help others. That makes you a real-life hero. You're also one of the most thoughtful men I know. Besides standing by me today, which no one has ever done for me before, you're kind to William. You make us both laugh, which isn't always easy to do."

Her lips flirted with a smile, before her eyes went soft with feeling. "You're also a wonderful lover."

"Okay," he said, confused.

"I'm trying to tell you that I love you."

Stunned, he sat back. "But this morning you said—"

"That I didn't? I lied."

What was he supposed to do with that?

After a long silence, Sam gave him a sideways look. "I knew I shouldn't tell you."

"Look, I really like you, Sam." More than he'd ever liked any woman, including his ex. He wasn't about to delve any deeper into his feelings than that.

"But you don't love me. You've always been honest about that. It's okay."

Her bright smile didn't fool him. He'd hurt her, which proved what a bad bet he was. "What do we do now?" he asked.

"Go our separate ways."

Adam wasn't sure he wanted that, but for her sake, it seemed the best route to take.

At the door, he shrugged into his jacket and tried to summon up something fitting to say. Nothing came to mind, and he settled for a bland good-bye. "Take care, Sam."

As he crossed the porch, the deadbolt clicked loudly behind him.

23

"I f you don't get your head on straight, you'll blow your interview," Rafe advised as Adam and the rest of the crew laid out their turnout gear for the evening ahead.

Adam all but snarled. It had been four days since Sam had dropped the "L" bomb and put him out to pasture. Since then, he'd learned that he'd passed the written part of his promotion requirement. Then he'd taken and passed the physical test. The final hurdle, the interview, was scheduled for mid-morning tomorrow, after his shift ended.

Despite the good news, he couldn't seem to shake off his foul mood. Couldn't even fake a smile.

"She dumped your sorry ass, didn't she? And after you helped her give the boot to her ex. Women." Rafe shook his head.

"You have it all wrong," Adam said.

"Her kid still too attached?"

As important as William was, his name hadn't come up in that particular discussion. "It's simple," Adam explained. "Her feelings for me are stronger than mine are for her." Or so he assured himself. "You know how that goes."

His buddy looked skeptical. "You sure about that? In the nine-plus years I've known you, I've never seen you like this. Man, you are so whipped."

Adam gave him the evil eye but didn't argue.

"I knew it." Rafe shook his head. "You'd better figure out what you want, or I just might have to take you out back and put you out of your misery."

SAMANTHA HAD JUST PULLED up the driveway after dropping William at school Wednesday, when Betty's sedan rolled to a stop in front of the house. She'd returned from Portland the day before.

Eager to see her friend, Samantha quickly exited her own car and hurried toward Betty's. "Welcome back," she called out as Betty put her window down. "William and I missed you a lot."

"I missed you, too. I wish I could visit for a while and tell you about my trip, but I'm meeting friends for breakfast. These are for you."

She handed Samantha a cellophane-wrapped bouquet of flowers. "I thought they might cheer you up."

The entire town seemed to know Samantha and Adam had parted ways for good.

"Aren't you sweet. These are lovely. I'm doing okay, though." Samantha forced a happy expression to underline the words. Be sure to broadcast how well I'm doing.

"Of course you are. When are you and William coming over? I'd invite you this afternoon, only I'll be out, playing bridge."

"You sure are busy. How about Saturday afternoon?"

"It's a date." Betty smiled. "I'll have the cocoa and coffee ready. Adam's having his interview this morning."

Samantha hadn't heard but tried to look as if she had.

"I'm sure he'll be relieved to have that behind him." Betty rubbed her arms. Now that it was early March, the weather had turned, carrying a hint of spring. But it was still too chilly to leave the car window down for long. "I need to scoot. Oh, before I forget, what kind of car does your ex-husband drive?"

Samantha couldn't recall. "An older gray four-door, but I'm not sure about the make and model. Why?"

"When I took my morning walk earlier, I thought I saw him drive past your house."

A shiver that had nothing to do with the temperature ran down Samantha's spine. "As far as I know, Bhodi left town last Friday."

"Five days ago? Then it couldn't have been his car. Forget I mentioned it."

Certain her ex was long gone, Samantha did exactly that.

～

"WHY ARE YOU SAD, MOM?" William asked early that afternoon.

Perceptive little guy. "I'm tired." That was true.

"You need a nap."

"Now you sound like me." She summoned up a smile. "I'll have another cup of coffee instead. I've noticed you yawning several times. Maybe you need the nap."

"No! I want to go outside and work on my fort."

After school the day before, Douglas and Harper had come over to play. The boys had spent several hours in the back yard constructing the fort using branches and an old blue tarp Samantha had found in the basement.

"Of course. Put on your coat and hat."

By the time William raced through the door, she'd set a mug of this morning's leftover coffee in the microwave. While she waited, she watched her son out the kitchen window. Soldier-like, he marched into the fort. He seemed to be doing well.

She, on the other hand suffered from a bad case of the broken-heart blues. Never mind. Sooner or later, she'd get past this.

The microwave beeped. Coffee and a magazine in hand, she sat down at the kitchen table. But when her cell phone rang sometime later, the coffee had grown cold and the magazine remained unopened.

Jana. Samantha almost didn't answer. She was so close to tears these days, and she didn't want to break down in front of William. Because he was busy with his fort and she needed to talk to her friend, she picked up.

"All ready for knitting class tomorrow?" Jana asked.

"So ready. Now that I finished the sweater, I need a new project. Any suggestions?"

"How about a purse? By the way, everyone missed you last week."

So much had happened since then that a week seemed a lifetime ago.

"How are you doing?" Jana asked.

Samantha hated her friend's solicitous tone. "You don't have to tiptoe around me. I'm strong and I'll bounce back." And darn it, no more pity party. She sat up tall. "You'll see."

"Atta girl. Why don't I drive tomorrow?"

"Great. I'm going to hang up now and phone my mother. I haven't filled her in yet about Bhodi."

"That sounds like real fun. See you in the morning."

Samantha caught her mother during a lull at the store, a perfect time to talk. She briefed her about Jeff's new name and his strange beliefs, and explained about the legal document he'd signed. She didn't mention Adam. She didn't want her mother getting ideas or quizzing her. What was the point, when the relationship had ended?

Her mother reacted as expected. "I'm shocked, Samantha. I really thought Jeff, or should I say, Bodhi, wanted you and William back."

"Nope. He didn't want us, and we didn't want him."

Her mother updated her on the goings-on in Enterprise. When they finally disconnected, nearly an hour had passed.

William had been outside the whole time. Samantha peeked out the window, but didn't see him. Probably crawling around in his fort. She opened the back door and bracketed her mouth with her hands. "William!"

No answer. Maybe he'd fallen asleep in there. Not bothering with a coat, she tromped outside, hugging her arms against the chill.

He wasn't in the fort. Or anywhere else in the front or back yards. She even checked her car. Odd. No longer aware of the cold, she stalked around the neighborhood, calling his name.

Nothing.

With a growing sense of alarm, she recalled Betty's

comment about the car she'd noticed this morning. And mulled over Bhodi's easy conciliatory behavior when he'd said good-bye, and the unnerving darkness that had flickered in his eyes.

He'd signed away his parental rights, but he'd also stated he didn't believe in legal documents.

What if he'd never left town? What if Betty had seen his car earlier? He could have taken William from under Samantha's nose, while she chatted away on the phone.

Oh, dear God, no. Her legs almost buckled under her. Running now, she raced into the house, grabbed her cell phone and called Adam.

Never mind that he didn't want her love. She needed him.

24

After a grueling three-hour meeting with four members of the division's upper echelons, Adam was brain dead, but also proud of himself for being relaxed and confident during the interview. He felt sure he'd aced the thing.

Then again, you never knew. Next step—wait to hear back. Whenever that would be. No one had said.

His empty belly reminded him that he'd missed lunch. Needing food, he drove to Lucky Joe's. There he slid onto a barstool at the counter. This time of day, business was slow, and in no time, the server placed a burger with the works in front of him. Adam dug in and thought about Sam. She'd want to know about the interview, but the way they'd left things, she wouldn't hear it from him.

His appetite dampened, he set the burger down. He missed her the way he'd miss his right hand.

Rafe had told him to figure out what he wanted. Adam didn't even have to think about that. He wanted to explore the relationship, find out where it took them.

Would Sam be open to that?

Only one way to find out—head over to her place

and talk about it. The problem was, by now William was home from school.

Yeah, but he was a part of this.

Adam returned to his meal. In record time, he finished, paid, and headed out.

He'd just buckled up when his cell phone buzzed.

Sam, the screen showed. "Hey," he said. "I'm on my way over to talk to you."

She didn't seem to hear him. "William's missing. I think Bodhi took him."

Adam frowned. "But he left town almost a week ago."

"That's what I thought, but Betty saw his car drive past the house this morning. And now..." Her voice broke.

"Call the cops." The 4Runner roared to life. "I'll contact my guys, and we'll be right there."

ALERT to every sound and any movement or activity, Adam prowled the neighborhood in search of William. Equally vigilant, Rafe accompanied him.

If Bodhi had abducted that innocent little kid...

Adam was so incensed, and yeah, scared at the thought, that his hands cramped from fisting them hard. He would personally deck the a-hole.

He cared a hell of a lot about William. And Sam, waiting on pins and needles at home, where the police had instructed her to stay in case her son showed up.

Betty had interrupted a bridge game and rushed over, along with Jana and the knitting group. While they offered support at home, Adam, Rafe, and a bunch of their crewmates combed the area.

The police were out looking, too. They didn't usually search for a missing adult this soon, but kids were different. They'd looked up Jeff Jones's license plate number, and were searching both here and on the roads.

"Where did you take him, you bastard?" Adam muttered through clenched teeth.

Rafe placed his hand on his shoulder. "Easy there, buddy. We don't know that Bhodi has him."

True, but tell that to Sam. Watching her as she'd paced, pale and frantic, wearing a trench through the house, Adam had vowed to do everything he could to bring her son back safely.

"Between us and the police, we'll find him," Rafe said.

Adam held on to that.

The afternoon wore on, and the sun inched toward the horizon. Exiting a small grove of trees some distance from Sam's house, he shaded his eyes and slowly panned the area. A shaft of rosy light shone on the roof of Betty Randall's barn.

The barn.

Wouldn't that be ironic, with Betty over at Sam's? Adam squinted at the barn door. He thought the latch hung open, but from this distance he couldn't be sure.

He moved closer for a better look. Yep, unlatched. He had a strong hunch Betty hadn't left it that way. He strode forward.

"Where are you headed, man?" Rafe asked, racing to catch up.

"To Betty's barn, where she keeps the horses."

The hinges creaked when Adam widened the door, and the animals nickered softly. He spotted William right away, fast asleep on the hay bale.

Exhaling a huge breath, Adam scooped the little guy up and held on tight.

"Adam." William yawned as he slowly came awake. "I falled asleep."

"You did, and your mom is worried sick. A lot of people are. We had no idea where you were." He didn't want to let go of the boy, but he needed to call Sam.

On the same wavelength, Rafe dug his own cell phone out of his pocket. "You contact Sam, I'll take care of the others."

She picked up on the first ring. "Adam?"

"There's someone here who wants to talk to you. Hold on, while I put this thing on speaker mode." That done, he nodded to William to go ahead.

The boy yawned again. "Hi, Mom."

"William!" Sam choked out a relieved sob. "Oh, sweetie, I'm so glad to hear your voice."

Adam's eyes filled. He squeezed the bridge of his nose. That stopped the urge to cry, but not the feelings crowding his chest—his heart—with love.

Love.

He loved Sam. He also loved William.

Whoa. He sank heavily on the hay bale.

Sam was still talking to her son. "Where have you been?"

"In the barn with Cocoa and Gordy. I couldn't find Mrs. Randall so I unlatched the door and came in by myself. I didn't bring any carrots, but the horses were awful happy to see me. Then I climbed onto the hay bale and falled asleep."

"I *knew* you needed a nap."

Eager to reunite Sam with her son, Adam gestured at William. "Say good-bye to your mom, sport, and I'll take you home."

25

With Adam, his crewmates, two police officers, Betty, and the knitting group, Sam's living room was too packed to move. Yet, as she rushed toward William, the group somehow parted to let her through.

Tears flowed freely down her face as she hugged her son tight. "I am so mad at you," she said, showering kisses on his face. "Don't you ever go off by yourself again without telling me first."

"Stop kissing me, Mom. I won't."

Still holding him and sniffling, her eyes wet and bright, she looked at Adam. "Thank you."

A big lump had formed in his throat. Unable to speak, he nodded.

The cell phone of one of the officers rang. He listened then disconnected. "We located Jeff Jones at his home, ma'am. He had nothing to do with this."

"I know that now," Sam said. "Thank you for your help."

After satisfying themselves all was well, the officers left. Everyone else hung around, teasing William and being extra nice to Sam.

"Knowing Bhodi wasn't involved makes up for a

lot," Sam said in a voice only loud enough for Jana's and Adam's ears. "So much that I'm finally ready to forgive him."

Adam couldn't hide his surprise. "No kidding?"

"This might sound weird, but suddenly all the bad"—glancing at William, she broke off—"the emotions I've carried around for three years are gone. I'll email Bhodi later and tell him."

No doubt her ex would be pleased.

"How does it feel to let go of the negative stuff you held onto all this time?" Jana asked, wearing a curious expression.

Sam looked pensive for a moment. Then she smiled. "Really good. Freeing."

William tugged on her sleeve. "Mom, I'm hungry."

"No wonder," she said. "It's past dinnertime. How about pizza for everyone?"

Adam spoke before anyone else could. "Sure, but you and I need to talk. Now. Alone." He clasped Sam's hand.

Betty, his buds, and the knitters nudged each other and gave him speculative looks. Ignoring them, Adam locked gazes with Sam. Her eyes softened as they always did, and his chest filled with sweetness.

"Go on, you two," Betty said. "I'll step outside and call in the pizza order."

All but salivating over this interesting turn of events, she was no doubt eager to spread the news. Let her. Adam nodded, tugged Sam into her office, and shut the door.

"While I searched for William..." His voice broke, and he had to stop and clear his throat. "If anything had happened to him..." He teared up.

Sam started crying again. He grabbed onto her, and they held each other for a while. When he pulled himself together, he tipped up her chin in order to see her face.

"That's when I realized how much the little guy means to me."

"Oh, Adam, I—"

He held up his hand, silencing her. "When you called to say he was missing, I was about to come over. I've thought a lot about you and me. I want to explore this amazing thing between us."

Again she opened her mouth to speak, and again he silenced her. "There's more."

He had to clear his throat again. "Over the past few hours, I realized having you and William in my life is non-negotiable. I want you with me always. Because— now don't fall over—I love you."

Her eyes shone. "I think you mean that."

"It took me a little while to admit it to myself. Are you willing to give this thick-headed guy a chance?"

"Yes. Oh, yes." She threw her arms around him.

Laughing for pure joy, he hugged her hard. Then he kissed her.

Sometime later, a knock sounded at the door. Betty poked her head in. Adam didn't release Sam and didn't miss the woman's knowing look.

"The pizza will be here soon," she said. "Oh, and congratulations, you two."

"What did you do, stand at the door and listen?" Adam tried to frown, but he was too happy.

"We all did." With an unrepentant smile, the nosey woman opened the door wider, revealing the whole group, crowded around and grinning.

Adam rolled his eyes. "Be sure to spread the word that Sam and I are together, Betty."

"I'll get on that right after dinner."

"What about me, Adam?" William asked.

Adam let go of Sam and ruffled the boy's hair. "From now on, you, your mom, and I are going spend a lot of time together. If that's okay with you."

"It is!"

William jumped up and down and clapped, and laughter filled the air.

LATER, Samantha and Adam cleaned up the pizza mess and William headed upstairs to change into his pajamas. Suddenly Adam's cell phone rang. By the way he straightened up, she guessed it was important.

"Yes, sir," he said. "I will."

When he disconnected, he looked so solemn. Fearing his father had taken a turn for the worse, she bit her lip. "Is everything okay?"

"Better than okay." A huge grin replaced his serious expression. "That was Captain Comings. From now on, you can call me 'lieutenant.' I got the promotion."

"Was there ever any doubt?" She threw her arms around the man she loved. "I'm so proud of you."

"I feel pretty damn good myself." His eyes sparkled. "I can't wait to tell Pop tomorrow. Come with me when I visit him. It's time he met my woman."

His woman. Samantha liked the sound of that. She nodded. "Should we bring William along?"

Adam scrubbed his hand over his face. "Richard isn't the easiest man to be around. Let's save that for later. This time, it'll be just you and me."

"All right. When I do my baking in the morning, I'll make an extra half-dozen muffins, just for him."

"He'll like that."

26

"I've never been in a 4Runner before," Samantha said as she and Adam drove toward his father's house in the gray gloom after dropping William at kindergarten. "It's nice and roomy."

"I like it. I like you better."

His smile melted her. After a tender and passionate night together, she felt loved and hopeful that maybe, just maybe, things would work out between them.

The icing on the cake had been William, acting as if seeing Adam in their kitchen in the dark hours of early morning was as normal as the sunrise.

"That's a nice shade of yellow," he added, nodding at the pullover under her open jacket. "Is it new?"

"This is what I've been slaving over in knitting class. I wanted to wear something bright and cheerful for your father."

Adam sobered. "About that. Don't think that because I let him know you were coming with me, he'll be warm and welcoming."

"I kinda got that the first ten times you told me." Adam seemed pretty uptight. "It can't be that bad. Are there any topics I should avoid?"

"I'll tell him about the promotion first. That'll put him in a decent mood and make him easier to get along with. Especially if you flash your prettiest smile and stick with surface stuff—the weather, baking. We won't stay long. I'll get you home in time for your knitting class. What's your next project?"

"I haven't decided yet. Listen, if things are going well with your dad and we decide to visit longer, I'll text Jana to go on without me."

"Noted." Adam pulled up to a modest cottage and braked to a stop. "We're here. Remember, he's hooked up to an oxygen tank. That can be unnerving when you first see him."

Samantha squeezed his tense hand. "Don't worry. This is going to be great."

~

ADAM DIDN'T SPEAK as he and Sam headed up the front walk to his pop's door. Sam had it right—he was plenty stressed about this visit. He wanted the old man to make nice today, which was why he'd phoned last night and given him a heads-up about Sam.

He hadn't even hinted about the promotion, and couldn't wait to see his father's face.

Nella had tacked her usual note on the door. No change from yesterday—his father had eaten, been shaved, and taken his meds. After knocking once, Adam opened the door and gestured Sam inside.

As always, the tube was on, but for once, the sound had been muted.

Adam grasped Sam's hand and brought her closer to his father. "Pop, this is Sam."

The old man looked her up and down. "Adam said you were a looker. He was right."

"Um, thanks." Sam blushed. "It's a pleasure to meet you, Mr. Healey."

"Call me Richard. Likewise." He eyed the bakery bag. "Is that for me?"

"As a matter of fact, yes." She handed him the bag.

Licking his lips, he rifled through the contents before choosing the one he wanted. After devouring it, he nodded at Adam. "You lucked out with this one, son."

With his father behaving himself, Adam breathed easier. "Don't I know it."

"There must be plenty of men after you," Richard commented. "Why in the world did you pick this guy?"

There was no humor in his voice, and Sam looked taken aback. "Off the top of my head, he's smart, handsome, and kind. I also happen to love him."

His father snorted. Her eyes widened in surprise.

Time to share the good news and turn things around. "Hey, Pop. I made the cut," Adam said. "You're looking at Guff's Lake Fire Department's new lieutenant."

Fully anticipating his father's pride and respect, he squared his shoulders.

But he didn't see a flicker of respect in Richard's eyes. No thumbs up or pleased smile, either, just a disbelieving shake of his grizzled head. "You must have snowed those fools just as you did Sam."

A punch to the chest would have hurt less. Refusing to flinch or react at all, Adam kept his expression carefully blank.

Sam gasped. "Surely, you don't mean that. Adam worked hard for this promotion. He's qualified, and he deserves it."

When the old man remained silent and unmoved,

she narrowed her eyes. "He also happens to be one of the finest men I've ever known."

"You're entitled to your opinion." Without another word, he unmuted the TV and amped up the volume.

She started to say something else, but Adam stopped her. "Don't waste your breath. Let's get out of here."

"You're right about your father," she said as soon as they stepped outside. "He's a very difficult man, and I pity him. But you...you have the patience of a saint."

Adam scoffed. "As a kid, I tried the patience of a saint. That's why Richard's the way he is, because of how I used to be."

She looked at him as if he were crazy. "You don't believe that."

"It's true."

"Baloney. Like you, me, and everyone else, your father is responsible for his own behavior."

Adam didn't buy that.

"Don't let him blame you for his actions and the choices he made and makes, and don't let him ruin your happiness."

"I won't," Adam pledged. Once he moved past the terrible disappointment of still not measuring up.

He was too shell-shocked on the drive home to make conversation. Sam must have sensed his need for silence because she let him be.

"Why don't you eat with William and me tonight?" she offered when he pulled up at her house.

He needed to lick his wounds alone. "We could both use a decent night's sleep, plus I should get some things done at my place," he said. "I'm meeting the captain at The Rogue for dinner tomorrow night to discuss my new job duties, so that's out, too. I'll call you. Say hi to your knitting friends."

He leaned across the seat for a kiss. Her sweetness and warmth washed over him, soothing his bruised soul.

"I love you," she sighed when he broke away.

"Love you, too."

OVER THE NEXT TWO DAYS, Adam caught up on chores at home, met with the captain, and mentally prepped for his new firefighter duties. He checked in with Sam, always hiding his pain. He also did a lot of thinking.

About his pop and their piss-poor relationship. As bad as Adam wanted to improve it, he couldn't force his father to care. With sudden clarity, he realized that no matter what he accomplished, the old man would always find him lacking.

That hurt.

Sam said he shouldn't blame himself for Richard's drinking and bitterness. That the responsibility for those choices lay with Richard, not Adam.

It took a little while for that to sink in. When it finally did, his jaw dropped. For the first time since Marcus's death, he was free from the burden of trying to please a man who chose to be miserable.

It had only taken him sixteen years to see things for what they really were. "Stupid idiot," he muttered, shaking his head.

His own words pulled him up short. For years, he'd accepted the label and other degrading names his father had laid on him. No more. He wasn't stupid, and for damn sure, no idiot. And as Sam had pointed out, he was a good man.

"I am a good man," he stated. Twice.

Saying it felt so great he laughed out loud.

And counted his blessings. He was a lieutenant at the Guff's Lake Fire Department, with a rosy future ahead. Sam loved him, and William probably did, too. Which made him the luckiest man alive.

Much of the credit for his mental turnaround belonged to Sam. She deserved a special thank-you, something she'd never forget.

Knowing exactly what he wanted to do, Adam called her. "Could you ask Betty to watch William for a little while tomorrow morning?"

"If she doesn't go to church. What's going on?"

"Tell you when I pick you up."

~

BEFORE HEADING to Sam's on Sunday morning, Adam stopped by his pop's with a muffin. In the seconds before he reached the door, the teeming rain drenched him. He paused in the threshold to wipe his feet and shake the raindrops off his coat. "Morning," he said.

Richard's sneer signaled a nasty comment coming. "Sam's a looker, but she must be blind and dumb to care about—"

"That's enough, Pop," Adam interrupted. "I love her and she loves me, so get used to it. I also love you, and even if you aren't proud of me for my promotion, I'm real proud of myself."

His father snorted and started to speak, but Adam cut him off again. "Here's your muffin." He dropped it on the TV table. "See ya."

Standing tall, he left. And headed for Sam's.

~

Rain pummeled the 4Runner so Samantha could hardly see out the window. "Where are we going?"

"Out for a drive."

"In this storm?"

"It's supposed to let up soon."

Adam seemed different from the last time they'd been together, but Samantha couldn't pin down what had changed. "You seem...lighter somehow," she commented.

"Is that right." Shrugging, he turned onto Kirkdale Road.

Some five minutes later, the rain stopped and the clouds began to disperse.

"You were right about the weather," she said.

At the sign for Guff's Lake, Adam veered off Kirkdale Road and followed the route to the lake.

Samantha frowned. "We're going to Guff's Lake?"

"Yeah." Adam parked in the deserted lot. "Let's take a walk."

Scattered puddles and mud made for an interesting trek. In the sunlight, the water droplets on the trees glittered like diamonds.

"I visited Pop this morning," Adam said.

"How was he today?"

"The same, but I'm not. I didn't let him put me down. I told him I'm proud of myself."

Samantha had never admired him more. "That's pretty amazing."

"And about time. He is who he is, and nothing I do will ever change him. Thanks to you, I finally get that."

"All I did was point out the truth."

"Which I couldn't see before." He grasped her hand. "I've been doing lot of thinking. If you can forgive Bhodi for all the crap he pulled, I can forgive my old man for treating me like dirt."

"Wow. You really have changed."

"And I feel damn good. Here we are." He stopped near a big tree.

Samantha noted the lofty branches, dripping and pale green with new life. "Isn't this the ash tree everyone talks about?"

"One and the same. Stand under it with me, so I can kiss you here. You know what that means, right?"

Her heart full, she nodded. "True and lasting love."

Solemn, he searched her face. "You in?"

"All the way."

Still holding hands, they moved under the tree. Adam pulled her into his arms and kissed her, and she knew they belonged to each other—now and forever.

THE END

THANK you for letting me share my stories with you!

There are 12 sexy firefighter books planned for the **Heroes of Rogue Valley: Calendar Guys**

IF YOU ENJOYED **MR. JANUARY**, help others find this book by recommending it to your friends and by writing a review. If you would like to know when my next release is available and other fun stuff, sign up for my newsletter here: www.annroth.net

VISIT ME AT FACEBOOK FACEBOOK.COM/ANN-ROTHAUTHORPAGE

Follow me on Twitter @Ann_Roth

Email me at ann@annroth.net
Visit my website www.annroth.net

THANKS, and until next time,
      Ann

PLEASE ENJOY this excerpt from **Mr. February**:

RAFE DONATO IS a senior firefighter well aware that loving a woman can destroy a man. He will never trust any female with his heart. Jillian Metzger is a talented potter whose biological clock is ticking. Ready to fall in love, get married and start a family, Jillian wants what Rafe cannot give.

"COME BACK HERE, POOH!" Jillian Metzger shouted as she sprinted across the uneven field adjacent to the cottage.

The Border collie had the gall to bark joyfully and skip over rocks and tree roots at a clip Jillian couldn't begin to keep up with.

To make matters worse, it started to rain. She hadn't taken the time to grab an umbrella, let alone a jacket—she'd simply darted out of the studio in hot pursuit. Not wise, considering temperatures in early March in Rogue Valley tended to be on the south side of chilly.

If and when she managed to catch Pooh, she was going to let her freeloading brother have it. Why couldn't JR keep an eye on his own dog? Because he'd gone out with Chelsea, frittering his day away when he should have been looking for a job.

Pooh was a good fifty yards ahead now, and Jillian quickly losing steam. She was on the verge of collapsing in exhaustion when the dog finally skidded to a stop. Tail wagging, Pooh changed course, trotting toward a man and woman standing slightly uphill, under a big umbrella. What were they doing here in the boonies on a rainy Wednesday morning?

Jillian lurched to a halt to catch her breath and pull herself together before they noticed her. A futile effort, given that she was a sodden mess. Leaning against the trunk of a lofty tree heavy with leaf buds, she tucked her dripping hair behind her ears with icy fingers.

She couldn't tear her gaze from them. What a striking couple. The dark-haired male, muscled and at least six feet tall, wore jeans, a light-blue sports shirt, and a black windbreaker that hugged his broad shoulders. His companion, with her shiny, stylish haircut and designer suit, stood close beside him under the umbrella.

Something about the guy seemed vaguely familiar, but before Jillian could place him, Pooh did the unthinkable—raced forward, jumped up, and planted her muddy paws on his powerful thigh.

"Get down, Pooh!" Jillian cried, pushing away from the trees and running again.

The big man didn't seem all that upset. He patted the dog and then brushed the mud off his jeans, which were neatly pressed, as was his shirt. Clutching the umbrella in both hands, his horrified companion quickly stepped out of reach.

The second his dark gaze met Jillian's, she recognized him. What red-blooded woman could forget those mesmerizing eyes, the strong jaw, and the slight hollows of his cheeks? She was about to come face-to-face with Rafe Donato, aka Mr. February in the Guff's Lake Fire Department calendar.

The calendar, part of the ongoing fund-raising drive for the department's benefit fund, had been released right before Christmas and featured twelve of the most gorgeous firefighters...

Drop-dead, movie-star-handsome Rafe looked even better in person than his photo—if that was even possible. Jillian's heart lifted in an appreciative sigh.

The calendar included certain important facts about each firefighter, stats any woman with a pulse would want to know. According to the details Jillian recalled—and with a calendar hanging on the wall in her studio, she was quite familiar with them—Rafe was single. At least he had been when the calendar was printed. By the intimate look from his lady friend, his status had changed.

"I'm sorry about Pooh," she apologized. "She's supposed to stay in the yard. Instead, the little scamp dug under the fence and lit out."

When Pooh had made her escape, Jillian had been in her pottery studio, creating pieces for one of her retail customers and for the Rogue Valley Arts Festival. If she hadn't decided to stretch her back and wander to the window, she wouldn't have noticed until the dog was long gone.

"My dog used to do the same thing."

Rafe flashed a smile, revealing dimples—holy cow, dimples—and extended his arm.

"Rafe Donato."

Wishing she'd dressed in something other than raggedy work clothes, Jillian wiped her palms on her threadbare, damp jeans before she shook his huge hand. His firm, warm grip engulfed her cold fingers, and his chocolate-brown eyes fixed intently on her.

Her knees wobbled. She glanced away. As attractive as Rafe was, she refused to go all weak and fluttery. He was already taken.

Even if he hadn't been, the ramrod straight posture, military-short hair, meticulously pressed shirt and jeans, and polished black boots screamed order and control. This was the kind of man who made life miserable for everyone around him. At eighteen, she'd left home to get away from that. She would never go back.

Pooh licked Jillian's hand. "Bad girl," she said, but the dog's innocent expression was hard to resist.

Rafe's girlfriend cleared her throat. "I'm Sonia Kaye, Rafe's architect." She started to extend her hand, but, after giving Jillian a quick once-over, offered her card and a perfunctory smile instead. "I should go, Rafe. I've seen enough for now, and I took plenty of photos. I'll be in touch."

"Let me walk you to your car." He held up a finger, signaling Jillian to wait.

Pooh wanted to follow the couple, but Jillian caught hold of her collar. "You're not going anywhere." The dog put wet-dog smell on a whole new level, and Jillian grimaced. "You need a bath."

With JR and Chelsea out, who knew where—they certainly hadn't said good-bye or left a note, but then, they never did—she would likely be the one doing the honors.

Rafe and his architect girlfriend moved in tandem up a gently sloping hill, toward the two expensive sedans parked on a dirt patch some distance away—one, a silver Mercedes, the other a gleaming navy convertible BMW.

Which belonged to him? The sleek BMW, Jillian guessed. It looked cleaner and somehow suited him.

Yep, the convertible was his. Rafe held the umbrella over Sonia's head while she climbed into a silver Mercedes. After flashing a flirty smile, she drove away, her tires churning up mud.

Rafe tromped back to Jillian. "Where do you and Pooh live?"

"Not far. On the other side of the field."

He nodded. "Cy Jackson's property."

"How do you know the name of my landlord?"

"I just bought the two-acre plot you're standing on, and I know everything about this area. Your cottage isn't more than a third of a mile from here, an easy walk, but this driving rain can make even a short distance seem like a long way. How about a lift?"

The offer surprised her. "We couldn't possibly. We're both wet and muddy, and Pooh stinks something terrible." She held her nose.

Rafe didn't argue with her. "You don't even have an umbrella. I do. I also happen to have a spare leash in the trunk of my car. Let me grab it, and I'll walk you and Pooh home."

JILLIAN WAS TALL, the top of her head almost level with Rafe's nose. That put her at about five-foot-ten. Long-limbed and slender, she could pass for a runway model—at least from what Rafe imagined. In baggy, wet clothes and dirty sneakers, he couldn't tell.

Her wet, shoulder-length blonde hair lay plastered to her head. Rafe remembered how cold her hand had felt in his. Any minute, her teeth would start to chatter.

"Here," he said, setting the umbrella down to shrug out of his lined windbreaker. "Put this on."

"But I'm a dirty mess."

"You're also freezing cold." He helped her into it then picked up the umbrella and held it over them. "Don't worry, it's washable. Zip up."

She did. The thing swam on her, which was kind of cute.

"How long have you lived on Cy's property?" he asked.

"For almost a year. Last month, I signed a lease for another year."

"We'll be neighbors, then—once I get my house built."

When not at the Guff's Lake Fire Department, Rafe spent his time managing his rental properties. He also kept an eye out for fixer-uppers, which he enjoyed re-modeling and selling. With the combined income he earned, he'd finally saved enough to build his dream home without emptying his bank account.

"Your own custom place? Lucky you. Sonia must be so excited."

"Because I hired her to design the house?"

"That and because you're a couple."

He laughed. "We're not together."

"Oh." Jillian looked surprised. "I assumed... You know."

"Getting romantically involved with my architect could be risky."

"Because if it didn't work out, you'd still need her help."

That and because as much as he liked women, and he liked them a lot, he didn't trust a single one enough to live with. Which wasn't quite true—he trusted his paternal grandma and a handful of female teachers from grade school and high school. But he preferred living alone. "Yeah."

Jillian nodded then angled her head. "You're a fire-fighter, right?"

"You've seen the calendar."

She blushed, adding much-needed color to her pale skin. "I have."

She had a generous mouth and fine, delicate features. "There's something on your chin," he noted, nodding at the gray glob stuck on the underside. The same stuff stained the cuff of her oversize sweatshirt. "And on your sleeve."

She touched the spot on her chin and rubbed at it, laughing self-consciously. "It's clay. I'm a potter."

"Ah. You do that full-time?"

"Yes. I sell to a couple of stores in the area an on-line. I'm also working on pieces for the Rogue Valley Arts Festival in Medford next month. Until recently, I also taught at the Artist Cooperative on the south side of town."

"You don't teach there anymore?"

"The school closed up shop last month. I'm getting ready to offer classes in my home studio."

"I never figured that little house with room for a studio."

"Actually, I use the outbuilding behind the cottage. With heat, electricity, and a skylight, it's perfect. I think it was originally designed as a workshop for household projects. I got permission from Cy to turn it into my pottery studio. My kiln is behind the building."

Rafe wondered how she made ends meet selling pottery and teaching classes. Having spent the first ten years of his life with his mom, whose sales from herbal concoctions and tie-dye T-shirts had often left them both hungry and moving in a hurry to escape eviction for non-payment of rent, he preferred a steady job with a regular paycheck, and money in the bank.

As they neared the cottage, Pooh woofed and strained at her leash.

"*Now* you want to get home," Jillian quipped. Under her breath, she added, "You'll change your tune when you realize you're about to get a bath."

Rafe chuckled, caught himself, and frowned. He wouldn't let this woman charm him.

Tibetan prayer flags were strung across the eaves over the porch. That and the aging VW van parked behind the hatchback in the gravel driveway reminded him of the years he'd lived with his mom.

Jillian frowned. "It's about time JR got back."

Rafe figured JR was her boyfriend. He wasn't about to ask—didn't want to know, but the words slipped out. "Who's JR?"

"My brother," she grumbled. "Thanks for walking me home, and for loaning me your jacket."

His unwitting gaze dropped to her plump, inviting lips. Jerking his attention to the jacket, he held out his hand for it.

"Let me clean it first. I'm happy to drop it off at the fire station later."

The guys were sure to razz him. He shrugged. "Sure. I won't be in again until Monday."

"Then you're a part-time firefighter?"

He shook his head. "I work Mondays and Tuesdays, two back-to-back, twenty-four-hour shifts. That's forty-eight hours a week, with five days off in between."

"Your days off sound nice, but isn't it dangerous, working such long hours with no break?"

"We each have a place to bunk at night, so I usually get some sleep. Even on busy nights, I manage all right. After eleven years, I'd better." Ready to leave, he gestured at the cottage. "Stay dry."

He turned away and strode back toward his property.

PLEASE ENJOY this excerpt from **Mr. March:**

FIREFIGHTER GUS VIGGIO needs to convince the stubborn great aunt who raised him and recently suffered a stroke to give up the house that has become too much for her. When she refuses, Gus enlists help from her flamboyant hairstylist, Wanda Lippman. The two women get along well, and Gus's great aunt just might listen to her. Wanda and Gus have each been hurt by love, and neither is ready to venture back into those dangerous waters anytime soon. But sometimes the heart knows best...

THE SECOND GUS VIGGIO offered his great aunt Polly a boost into his Jeep Cherokee, she shook her cane and fixed him with that stubborn *I'm not a helpless old lady yet* look that warned him to back off. God help him if he attempted to buckle her in.

Hands shoved into his jeans pockets, he stood by the open passenger door. Just in case. She wasn't as strong as she used to be, and those arthritic hands made even fastening the seatbelt difficult.

While he waited, he squinted against the sun, bright but not strong enough to take the chill out of the April morning. Almost overnight, spring had sprung in the Rogue Valley. Here in Guff's Lake, grass, shrubs and flowers, dormant through the winter, had made up for lost time and grown by leaps and bounds.

"My yard is mess," Aunt Polly lamented.

Once an avid gardener, she could no longer handle yard work. Gus had taken over the job, with occasional help from his father. "Dad and I will stop by and take care of it this weekend."

Maintaining the large front and back yards took a big chunk of time, but Gus didn't mind. He loved Aunt Polly dearly. When his mom had left, his great aunt had invited him and his dad to move in and had raised Gus as her own.

Years ago, they'd decided to dispense with the "great" label, respectively shortening their names to "Aunt Polly" and "nephew." Not that "aunt" cut it, either. She was more a mother and grandmother rolled into one. He would do anything for her. Anything.

Buckled in at last, Aunt Polly folded her hands in her lap. "What are we waiting for?" she said with an impish look. "Let's boogie."

He grinned at her word choice. "You're in a good mood today."

"On such a beautiful morning, how could I not be?" She slipped a pair of sunglasses over her bifocals. "Besides, it isn't every day my favorite nephew and two of his fellow firefighters take me to lunch at Ellen's."

The stuffy restaurant wasn't at the top of Gus's go-to list, but his aunt loved eating there, and his buds enjoyed her company, so they tolerated the place.

"Your *only* nephew," he reminded her, pulling on his Ray-Bans.

"If I had a dozen, you'd still be my favorite."

"Not favorite enough to take my advice."

Her lips thinned. "Don't you dare start in on me about my living arrangements, Augusto Frances Viggio. I'm perfectly able to take care of myself, and you know it."

The use of Gus's full name meant she was seriously irritated, but didn't change the fact he disagreed with her.

Insisting on independence, she lived alone in her big, old house. No amount of reasoning or cajoling had convinced her to downsize and move into an apartment in a retirement community.

She did allow him to chauffeur her around, thanks to a stroke ten months ago that had put an end to her driving. Gus didn't mind shuttling her where she needed to go—when he could. Between him and his dad, they managed.

"If and when I decide to leave, I promise to let you know," she added. "But don't hold your breath." Raising her chin, she changed the subject. "As I was saying, you are my favorite nephew. Who else can I rely on to take me to my weekly hair appointment with Wanda?"

Gus tabled the conversation about moving—for the moment. "No problem."

Tommie's Hair and Nails was an easy ten-minute drive from Aunt Polly's house. "I need to schedule an inspection at Tommie's. May as well set that up today."

"For the safety project?"

"That's the one."

Gus had been tasked with checking fire and smoke alarms in every commercial and multi-dwelling residential structure as well as updating computer diagrams with the safest routes into and out of each. Important information that was posted in every building for both civilians and emergency responders to use during emergencies.

Gathering and collating all that data in the town of

almost twenty-thousand people was taking more time than Gus had estimated. When he'd started ten weeks earlier, he'd promised the captain a finish date of early August. As tight as the deadline now seemed, he intended to deliver, even if it meant working off the clock.

No longer cross with him, Aunt Polly tilted her lips into a fond smile. "Not just anyone is strong and smart enough to be a firefighter. I'm so proud of you."

Gus's chest expanded. Not one for big displays of emotion, he gave a modest shrug.

"I can't wait to tell Wanda about lunch today," Aunt Polly said. "She'll be all ears. She's a darling, that one."

Darling wasn't the word that came to mind when Gus thought of Wanda Lipmann, who looked to be in her late twenties. He never knew what to expect when he saw her. Short and curvy, she wore her clothes bright and tight, and she changed her hair-style and color a couple times a month. Talk about unsettling.

They hadn't spoken much, except to say hi and bye when he brought Aunt Polly in and picked her up.

His aunt cast him a sly look. "If you'd get to know Wanda, you'd realize how special she is."

Gus rolled his eyes. "Stop right there. You are not fixing me up—now or ever."

"But it's been almost a year since your breakup with Delores."

"Denise," he corrected. "I'm way over her."

For sure. After she'd pressured him one too many times to get married, he'd decided to break up with her. Then Aunt Polly had had her stroke. "Trust me, if I had time, I'd be dating. I happen to have a lot on my plate."

Between working at the Guff's Lake Fire Department, looking after Aunt Polly, and running his one-man classic car restoration business, Gus was overbooked.

Not that he wanted to give up any of his responsibilities. His car business relaxed him and felt more like play. Currently, he was restoring a 1965 classic Lincoln. His customer had agreed to pay top dollar, with a bonus if he finished in time for the classic car show in mid-May.

Whipping off her sunglasses, Aunt Polly gave him the no-nonsense look that had always worked during her librarian days, her still-bright eyes serious behind the bifocals. "At thirty-two, you're not getting any younger."

"Don't hold back."

"Have I ever? It's time you found a wife and settled down. That should be your priority, but because it isn't, you need help. Mine."

She'd been after him to get married since the day he turned thirty, nagging him with a dogged determination that wouldn't quit.

Gus narrowed his eyes a fraction. "Stop."

"I will not." She sniffed. "Come October, I'll be eighty. I've earned the right to speak my mind."

"Like that's anything new. You know I'm not against marriage, but there's no guarantee it'll happen."

"Pish posh," Aunt Polly said. "Of course it will."

His parents had split up when he was seven, but he had good little-kid memories. Settling down and having two or three children appealed to him. But to date, every one of his serious relationships had gone south.

In matters of the heart, he'd begun to think he was just like his father. This apple hadn't fallen far from the tree.

Gus pulled onto Brewster Street, home to a dozen small businesses on the west side of town. Tommie's Hair and Nails salon was always buzzing, mostly with women, and judging by the number of cars parked in the salon lot, this morning was no different.

"This is a wash-and-trim appointment. I'll be done in about thirty minutes," his aunt said as opened the passenger door for her. "Since you need to schedule that inspection, you may as well wait inside."

Having just come off forty-eight hours—two back-to-back shifts—at the Guff's Lake Fire Department, with a couple calls in the dead of night, Gus planned to grab some quick Z's in the Jeep while Aunt Polly had her hair done. He'd deliver her to Wanda, schedule the inspection, then make a beeline for the Jeep.

Refusing his arm, she relied on her cane. In the sunlight, the sparkly *Tommie's Hair and Nails* sign on the door glittered. Gus ushered his aunt inside and removed his shades.

The half-dozen or so females in the process of manicures and haircuts stopped chattering and stared at him.

Every week he brought Aunt Polly here, but you'd think they'd never seen him in the salon. Maybe it was his size. Bigger than many men, he'd grown used to curious looks. Lately, more than usual, thanks to the firefighter calendar.

Feeling awkward, he nodded at Carol Sue, who had about ten years on him.

"Nice to see you, Polly. Hi there, Gus," she said, batting her lashes at him.

"Hey," he replied, courteous but not too friendly.

A flirt and a gossip, Carol Sue lived to spread rumors. Here in Guff's Lake, information spread faster than a forest fire in summer. Gus preferred to stay out of her stories.

"Who do I talk to about scheduling a salon inspection?" he asked.

"That would be either Tommie or Wanda. Tommie's out just now, but Wanda is here. I'll let her know you and Polly have arrived. Help yourselves to coffee. The one with the orange band is the decaf you want, Polly. The other is leaded. Enjoy." She sashayed off.

Gus got Aunt Polly settled on the sofa and brought her a decaf with sugar and creamer. He filled a Styrofoam cup with the leaded stuff and sat in a chair. A few sips in, the "Employees Only" door at the rear of the salon opened. Wanda and two stylists stepped inside.

Sticking close to the door, all three glanced his way and whispered. God knew what they were saying. As long as it didn't go on too long, Gus didn't care.

He took another few sips of coffee before Wanda started forward.

～

POLLY BECKER RANKED among Wanda's favorite customers. She wasn't so comfortable with Polly's great nephew.

At six foot four and two hundred thirty pounds—details everyone who owned a Guff's Lake Fire Department calendar knew—Gus, aka Mr. March, was a strikingly handsome man. All solid muscle, he was built more like a super-fit linebacker than a firefighter. The piercing green eyes and short, light-brown hair with a hint of red didn't hurt, either. Looking at him, a woman would have to be dead not to have heart palpitations.

The calendar, sold to raise money for the station's benefit fund, had turned Gus and the eleven men featured into local celebrities.

Nadia, a stylist and close friend Wanda had been chatting with in back, elbowed her. "He always drops Polly off and leaves," she said in a low voice. "Carol Sue says he wants to talk to you today. I wonder why?"

"What does it matter, as long as I'm in the same room as him?" murmured Rochelle, Wanda's second closest friend. She worked from noon to closing on Wednesdays, but had come in early to accommodate a customer. She fanned herself. "He's even more gorgeous in person."

In place of his usual T-shirt, jeans and weathered leather jacket, he'd switched it up in a pressed blue shirt, dark pants and polished black oxfords. He looked good in dress clothes, but he looked equally fine in casuals.

"Maybe I'll move my schedule around and start working early on Wednesdays." Rochelle gave Wanda a sideways glance. "Unless you have dibs on him?"

Currently, both Rochelle and Nadia were single and in the market for a boyfriend. Wanda frowned. "Tommie depends on you to work late Tuesdays and Wednesdays. And don't forget, I'm taking a break from men."

Her friends shared a look. "You say that every time you go through a breakup," Nadia pointed out. "Until some cute guy asks you out. Then you're off and running again."

"After I've turned down every guy who asked me out the past six-and-a-half months? If that isn't serious, I don't know what is."

She refused to date until she figured out how to win and hold a man's love with more than good sex.

She had the sex part down but not the rest, and her heart had been broken more times than she could count.

The latest split with Larry had hurt almost as much as losing Wayne ten years earlier. In hindsight, she realized much of the pain stemmed from her seriously wounded pride. She'd tried her best to keep Larry interested but had failed. Yet again. She didn't think she could survive one more breakup.

"To clarify," Rochelle said, "you're not interested in Gus Viggio."

"Right."

Even if a mere glance at the man caused a spike in her pulse rate, he'd never given her more than a brief greeting and a cursory glance. A good thing, too. Otherwise, she might be tempted to forget she'd sworn off guys, proving her friends right.

"Polly's waiting for me," she said. "And apparently so is Gus."

Curious as she was about what he could possibly want, she paused and fluffed her layered, purple-streaked, blond hair—a far cry from its dull-brown natural color. She strutted forward, her teal, three-inch ankle boots clicking smartly across the tile floor. The walk had taken years to perfect.

As she drew closer, Gus pushed to his feet. His great aunt had raised him right.

"Morning, Polly," Wanda said, with a warm smile.

The older woman beamed. "I like your hair, Wanda. Those purple streaks are fun. And what a snazzy outfit."

"Thanks." Wanda smoothed her short-sleeve, lavender tee over her hips. Even with the three extra inches of the ankle boots, she was only five feet six.

She tilted her head back a little to greet the firefighter. "Hello, Gus."

He nodded, his expression impossible to read, and gave her a once-over from her head to the hint of cleavage, courtesy of the low scoop neck, where his gaze lingered a beat longer than an uninterested man's should have. Then past her flared, teal skirt to her black leggings.

Pride surged through her. As with her walk, the cutting-edge hairstyles and clothing had never been natural to her. Neither was being bubbly and talkative. But wanting to be noticed and liked by men, even though she'd temporarily sworn off them, she'd adjusted. Her efforts had paid off. Getting a date when she wanted one was never a problem, and both male and female customers kept coming back.

Proving Cindy right, for once.

"I'm told you're the one to see about scheduling a safety inspection," he said, his deep, sexy voice vibrating through her.

Safety inspection—of course. A little part of her had assumed he wanted information of the personal kind. What a relief he didn't. Or so she assured herself. Yet something inside her deflated a fraction. "I'm the one, all right."

"Do you have any time Monday?"

"We're closed that day, but I guess that'd work."

"If you're closed, who'll let me in?"

"Either Tommie or me."

Likely Wanda. Tommie had just turned sixty-five and decided to retire at the end of September. Wanda wanted to buy the business and the building—provided she saved up enough for the down-payment necessary to secure a loan. Although she still needed a fair chunk of change, she'd assured Tommie that when the time came, she would have the required funds.

The past few months, Tommie had been teaching her the ins and outs of running the salon, and slowly giving Wanda more responsibility.

"Your aunt should be ready to go in about a half hour," she told Gus. "You can pick her up then."

"He's going to wait here today." Polly showered him with a fond grin. "Then he's taking me to lunch at Ellen's."

No wonder he'd dressed up. "Lucky you." Wanda sighed.

She'd always wanted to try the upscale restaurant, but not one of her boyfriends had ever taken her there. "Have a seat in the waiting area, Gus. I'll bring her to you when we finish. Come on, Polly, let's make you gorgeous."

She offered her arm, but Polly rebuffed her. Thanks to her shoes, Wanda stood some two inches over the woman. She also moved a lot quicker. She slowed way down, and they made their way to her station across the way.

Or tried.

Polly dug in her heels and waved her cane at Gus. "Aren't you coming with us?"

"My station is small, and there's no place for you to sit," Wanda pointed out. "You'll be more comfortable in the waiting area."

So would she. If he hovered around, she wouldn't be able to relax.

"Nonsense. He'll bring a seat with him," Polly insisted. "I want him to see what you do."

"Aunt Polly..."

Wanda didn't understand Gus's warning look."

Lips compressed, Polly turned away from his gaze.

While he returned to the waiting area to grab a chair, Wanda helped her into the salon chair. She fastened a large plastic smock around Polly's neck, gently tipped her back to wash her hair, and wondered what her customer was up to.

Coming soon! **Mr. April:**

When firefighter Owen Ayers agrees to let freelance writer Hallie Sawyer shadow him to gather information for her article about Guff's Lake Fire Department, he assumes the task will be easy. Instead, sharing his time with the plucky brunette proves challenging—and not just on a professional level. Burned by a failed marriage and wary of getting involved, Owen is irresistibly drawn to Hallie. After suffering through the unimaginable pain of losing her fiancé and unborn daughter, Hallie is determined to rebuild her life by avoiding relationships and focusing on her career. But sexy Owen threatens to breach her protective shell. The healing power of love just might save them both.

ALSO BY ANN ROTH

Book 2 The Pilot's Woman
Book 3 Ooh, Baby!
Book 4 The One I Love

Miracle Falls
Book 1 Christmas in Miracle Falls
Book 2 Dream a Little Dream
Book 3 It Had to Be You
Book 4: You're the One That I Want

Saddlers Prairie
Book 1 Since I Fell for You
Book 2 I'll Be There
Book 3 Until There Was You

ABOUT THE AUTHOR

Ann Roth is an award-winning author of 40-plus contemporary romance and women's fiction novels, as well as novellas and numerous short stories. Her first novel was published in 2000 by Harlequin Special Edition and was nominated by *Romantic Times* as best first book. Ann lives with the love of her life in the Greater Seattle area and enjoys creating flawed characters and putting them in challenging situations that help them grow and ultimately find love— whether or not they're looking for it.

Find out about new releases!
Sign up for my newsletter

Or visit my website www.annroth.net

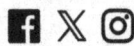